Beyond *All* Expectation

ABNER HAUGEN LIBRARY
Zumbro Lutheran Church
624 Third Ave SW
Rochester MN 55902

Beyond *All* Expectation

JOHN MARK

THE AUTHOR AS "John Mark" IS A PSEUDONYM FOR:
MARK EVAN SPECKHARD
16326 W. INDIANOLA AVE.
GOODYEAR, AZ. 85395

Copyright © 2017 John Mark.

All rights reserved. No part of this book may be reproduced, stored, or transmitted by any means—whether auditory, graphic, mechanical, or electronic—without written permission of the author, except in the case of brief excerpts used in critical articles and reviews. Unauthorized reproduction of any part of this work is illegal and is punishable by law.

ISBN: 978-1-4834-6799-3 (sc)
ISBN: 978-1-4834-6798-6 (e)

Library of Congress Control Number: 2017905010

Any people depicted in stock imagery provided by Thinkstock are models, and such images are being used for illustrative purposes only. Certain stock imagery © Thinkstock.

Scripture quotations are from the New Revised Standard Version Bible, copyright ©1989 the Division of Christian Education of the National Council of the Churches of Christ in the United States of America. Used by permission. All rights reserved.

Lulu Publishing Services rev. date: 5/9/2017

In Grateful Recognition

My wife, Myrna, has shown incredible love and patience that have sustained me during the development of this book. My children, Steve, Mark, and Jennifer, have been a constant source of love. Jennifer has assisted in guiding the manuscript on its path to publication. To each of you and many more who have shown me love, I owe you much. You have my gratitude beyond measure.

Contents

	Prologue	ix
CHAPTER ONE	So This Is Faith	1
CHAPTER TWO	We Were Accountable	8
CHAPTER THREE	We Are Forgiven	19
CHAPTER FOUR	Grace, a Gift from God	35
CHAPTER FIVE	We Say Thank You	46
CHAPTER SIX	We Are Inspired	55
CHAPTER SEVEN	Interactions with God	65
CHAPTER EIGHT	The Church Spreads the Good News	74
CHAPTER NINE	God Answers Prayers	84
CHAPTER TEN	Hans Shares the Good News with Anthony	102
CHAPTER ELEVEN	Anthony Shares It Further	111
CHAPTER TWELVE	Now It's Our Turn	118
	Epilogue	123

PROLOGUE

God, life, and lessons learned told from the humble surroundings of our kitchen table. Imagine the kitchen, and you will notice a young boy standing near the table, his hand resting comfortably on its surface. It's Hans, thirteen years old and feeling quite grown up. More than anything, he wants to tell you about his world, which is to say, about his home. He has the advantage of youth. Clear eyesight, without the overlay that comes with age. He tells it best in his own words.

CHAPTER ONE

So This Is Faith

Our kitchen table is the safest place on earth. I know that sounds strange. But let me tell you about the safety at our kitchen table, and you can be the judge.

It's a huge table, to be sure. But then our kitchen is huge as well. My parents moved into this house after they were married, barely a year before I was born—in 1525 to be exact. The house is large, with so many rooms that we are able to take in university students as boarders. My father is a professor at the university in our town. And the students are eager to hear my father share his insights or elaborate on his lectures as they gather each noon for dinner at the kitchen table.

My father sits at the head of the table. He's a kind and thoughtful man and totally in charge. The students love to question him, and the bravest may even debate with him. Meanwhile, my father guides the discussion and always has the final word. He's the professor, after all. As I watch and listen to him, I can feel the security that he brings to my life, the safety that I feel at the kitchen table.

Across from me but nearer to my father sits Nicholas, one of the many students gathered at our table. Nicholas loves to probe and question and may even push the limits—sometimes with success and sometimes not so much. In fact, humiliation is not uncommon when Nicholas pushes too hard. Yet through it all, he benefits, learns, and gathers much.

I have come to admire Nicholas. Whenever I glance at him, he welcomes me with the hint of a smile or slight arch of an eyebrow as though to assure me that we are in this together, as if to say, "Did you catch that? Did you hear what your father just said?" And best of all, when he can, Nicholas will find me later and explain for me the issues that were discussed that day. Most of what I learn, I owe to Nicholas.

My mother sits near me, at our end of the table. You can imagine how busy she is, managing this household. But her love surrounds us, supports us, and reassures us of our acceptance. She provides an element of safety that is equal to my father's, though of a different nature. Because she is so busy, her love for me is often best expressed when we sit together at the kitchen table.

Across from me, but closer to my mother, sits Aunt Lena, or Aunt Magdalena, I should say in introducing her. She is a hardworking, gentle soul. She helps my mother, which keeps her busy enough. But Aunt Lena always has time for a smile and a kind word. Each time she glances at me, her smile warms me through and through. She cares deeply for us all; that is evident. But she gives special love and attention to her namesake, little Lenchen, sitting close beside her.

Lenchen, just nine years old, is now my closest sibling. I had a sister, Elizabeth, who died when she was two. People said she died from the plague. I barely remember her because I was only four at the time. Then came Lenchen, Magdalena by birth. No question, she has won my heart. Despite the difference in our ages, we are the best of friends. We love to compete; we plot and scheme and wait to see who can come out better than the other.

To know Lenchen best, you have to see her in action and watch her at play. Her light-brown hair braided, shining. Her blue eyes full of mischief, laughing. Teasing her younger brothers and her little sister, chasing them but also coming to their rescue. As her older brother, I sometimes stand near, quiet, thoughtful, watching the fun, and in the watching, becoming part of it.

I worry about Lenchen because she is so often ill. But then, soon, Lenchen is well again, and the mischief and the joy take over, and all thought of illness is forgotten. But not so easily forgotten by me—because I know what can happen in our world, what did happen to Elizabeth. So I am grateful when I see her on the mend, but I am never totally at ease. My little Lenchen. How does she have such an influence on me? How can we see each other so clearly and understand each other so well?

Lenchen at the dinner table, whispering with the others, talking quietly with Aunt Lena, who adores her namesake. Lenchen occasionally looks over at me, but often all I get is a bob of her little head.

In the evening, the house grows quiet. Yet in the stillness, the household never loses its sense of purpose, the tension of debate, the reverence of family, and the respect students have for my father. It is certain that the next day will bring renewed discussion, new insights, and intriguing questions that will lead to ever new debate.

This is our household. In the center of it is the kitchen table—a table filled with active give and take, of table talk. Every noon, along with our meal, we get a helping of grace, mercy, and peace, of love and faith. My father and the students will scratch the surface of whatever the topic of the day may be and then view it from many sides. The meaning does not change. Yet with each encounter, we get to know it better, just as we truly get to know a person well through many encounters, with the chance to see the person from different viewpoints. My father says that truth is not a block of stone; it is a shining light that must be examined from many sides.

Take today, for example. The dinner table was strewn with anecdotes of those who had shown faith to a remarkable degree, examples from throughout the ages. I was fascinated. I feel like I have been surrounded by faith all my life, but I still find faith difficult to grasp at times.

When I caught up with Nicholas shortly after dinner, I asked him, "Nicholas, please give me an example of faith. Help me know what it really means."

Nicholas smiled at my eagerness, thought for a moment, and then answered, "Just imagine the Virgin Mary, Hans. Like you, she is very young. Perhaps a little older than you, but probably still in her midteens. She's just an ordinary girl. And then she sees an angel standing by her side who calls her by name. And even more remarkable, she hears the angel say, 'You will bear a child.'

"Just think, Hans. Mary knows how pregnancy occurs, and as a virgin, she senses the impossibility. Many translators give her response as, 'How *can* this be? For I am a virgin.' A response filled with disbelief, doubt. But the account in Greek, which is the earliest source for this story, is probably better translated, 'How *will* this be? For I am a virgin.' Not a matter of doubt but of acceptance. A request for instruction. Saying, in effect, please tell me the next step. The angel responds, 'The Holy Spirit will make this happen, and the child you bear will be called the Son of God.'

"For Mary, this is stranger still. As a virgin, she will bear a child. Astounding. Even more astounding, he will be the Son of God. Hans, imagine how you and I would respond, if we could even think of anything to say. But Mary doesn't hesitate at all. Quiet, humble, confident, she replies, 'Here I am. Let it be with me exactly as you say.' So there you have it, Hans. That's faith."

I thought for a moment, but I found Mary's reaction hard to understand. "Tell me, Nicholas. Truly. How could Mary be so calm?"

Nicholas briefly smiled again, understanding my difficulty. "She was young, Hans. She had an open mind, and that made all the difference."

Nicholas paused for a moment and then said, "Let me give you a comparison that will make you feel more at home. About six months earlier, an angel came to a man named Zechariah, who was to become the father of John the Baptist. Zechariah was old, as was his wife, Elizabeth. They had never had a child, and they were convinced by this time that they never would. While Zechariah was serving as a priest, an angel appeared to him, and he was terrified. The Bible says, 'fear overwhelmed him.' Wouldn't you be terrified? Wouldn't that be a normal reaction for any adult?"

This reaction certainly did sound more familiar to me, and I nodded. Meanwhile, Nicholas continued. "The angel said, 'Don't be afraid, Zechariah, for your prayer has been heard. Your wife, Elizabeth, will bear you a son, and you will name him John.' Zechariah was not so easily convinced. In fact, he was filled with doubt, and he replied to the angel, 'How will I know that this is so? For I am an old man, and my wife is getting on in years.' He wanted proof—no taking this on faith."

I shrugged, suggesting I understood completely where Zechariah was coming from. Nicholas smiled again, understanding my reaction. "The difference is that Mary was willing to consider these things with an open mind. She was not a child. But she had the open, accepting mind of a child. As you would expect of most adults, Zechariah was terrified by the sight of an angel. When the angel told Zechariah that Elizabeth would have a child, which was a miracle in his eyes, Zechariah wanted proof—a common adult response. Mary, on the other hand, while perplexed by the sight of the angel, was not terrified or afraid. When the angel told Mary she would have a child, which was an even greater miracle because she was a virgin, Mary thought it over and replied, 'Let it happen just as you said.' A response in keeping with the open, accepting mind of a child."

I looked thoughtful, but after a pause, I nodded. Nicholas looked at me, his manner kind, accepting. Then he said, "The most important thing about having faith is for you to be willing to see and to listen with an open mind. You can't think or reason your way into accepting a miracle. You can only approach it with an open mind, wiping out all the objections that fill the mature mind of an adult. Zechariah's wife, Elizabeth, recognized this as she later spoke to her cousin Mary, congratulating her, 'Blessed is she who believed' what the angel had told her. We each would like to have such a strong faith. We too would feel blessed to have the faith of Mary. If we look closely at Mary, and her open-minded acceptance, we see the path that we can follow if we wish to find such faith."

I was even more thoughtful now, expectant, yet not knowing where this would lead. It took me a moment, and then I ventured, "If I have faith, what exactly should I have faith in?"

Nicholas was ready, and he answered, "Later, Zechariah gives us a hint about where this is heading. Zechariah talks about the role his newborn son John would play in preparing people for the coming of the Messiah, of Christ. He tells us that in his mercy, God has sent us a savior. Then Zechariah becomes poetic, 'By the tender mercy of our God, the dawn from on high will break upon us, to give light to those who sit in darkness and in the shadow of death, to guide our feet into the way of peace.'"

I was lost in thought, but then I looked sharply at Nicholas. "Those are beautiful words, but what do they really mean? What's Zechariah telling us?"

Nicholas replied, "It's a prediction. For Zechariah, it's the story of a lifetime." He paused, and then he smiled. "Just wait. There's so much more to come."

CHAPTER TWO

We Were Accountable

At dinner the next day, I glanced around the kitchen table, enjoying the hum of conversation, the occasional laughter, the familiar faces. Then my mind drifted back to the day before, focusing on Zechariah. What did his prediction mean? How would it be fulfilled? While I sat there half attentive, half musing, I found myself joining in the laughter that washed over us from my father's end of the table. He shows a sense of humor that endears him to his students, and of course, to us. While he never loses the central point of the discussion, he injects humor that sharpens the debate, making each point more memorable.

Laughter makes our kitchen table special. When we laugh together, we can feel the bond that links us. It's a bond that is lighthearted, yet particularly strong. We acknowledge in a special way our joyful acceptance of each other, acceptance that both cheers us and makes us feel secure. Amid the laughter, our kitchen table becomes an even safer place. We do not need to be on guard; we only need to enjoy each other. Wherever in this world we laugh together, we strengthen the bond between us.

It's strange that food has much the same effect on us. It bonds us. This is strange in a way because food is an inevitable presence at our table, at most kitchen tables. In large part, it defines the purpose for the kitchen table. And so it seems surprising to me that food, something so natural, so universal, can form such a powerful bond between us. We feel a kinship with our fellows, each of those eating at our side. More than that, eating with each other in a group defines the group as well. In a very real way, gathering together for a meal at our kitchen table makes us feel distinct from the world around us. We feel special in a way. We feel safety in this kinship.

There are so many examples of the way that food forms a bond. Imagine students entering a school dining hall. With food in hand, they head to a table. They may come individually or two or three together. Soon the table is almost full. These are a scattering of students who have gathered at an empty table. Then they begin to eat, and at that point, they are a group...a group of students eating lunch together. From the moment they begin eating, anyone approaching the table to take the one remaining seat is apt to say, "May I join you?" It is addressed to the group. The act of eating together has brought definition to the students who may have come individually but now are seen as a group. It is eating together that has done this. If they were in the library studying at a table, a student approaching the table would be apt to take the one remaining seat without a word, or merely ask, "Is this seat taken?"

And so eating together at our kitchen table has this power, though even more so. A new student who joins our table is rapidly assimilated into the group. Very soon he will come to the table at mealtime with the comfortable sense of belonging. Food has that power.

Yet the real safety of our kitchen table comes from quite a different direction, on a different level. We feel safe as we find answers to the issues that intrigue us or may trouble us. As we address the problems of the world at large or those that are confined to our little world, big problems or small, we search for answers that will make us feel more secure. And at the kitchen table we find mutual support in this effort. Take today for example. As I was relaxing in the laughter and enjoying the food, a question drifted down from my father's end of the table. "Where does evil come from?" At first all was quiet, and then there was active debate.

When I talked with Nicholas later, I could sense his mind was still immersed in the discussion that had followed. I was keen to get him off that track, and as I greeted him, I said, "I've been waiting to hear you explain Zechariah's prophecy."

Nicholas smiled in response. "Actually, evil is the beginning of the answer." Nicholas was looking at me and could sense immediately that I was not eager to head in that direction. He put a hand on my forearm as he continued. "This is the dark side, Hans. This is the side that no one wants to talk about, not even think about."

I was upset as I replied, "I get so angry with God when I think of all the evil in this world. Especially when I think of a young child dying from a terrible disease. Or anyone dying from starvation. Why does God let that happen?"

Nicholas was clearly sympathetic as he answered me. "I know, Hans. There are so many evils in this world…disease, starvation, devastating acts of nature, wars." He paused for a moment; the list was so long. Then he continued. "But as we try to deal with evil, the first step is to see where evil comes from. And if we look carefully at evil, we may see that God is actually on our side."

"Really?" I said in a tone that showed I found this difficult to accept. But in any case, I was ready to know more about evil, and I asked, "So where does evil come from? Let's start with that."

Nicholas responded immediately. I think he was afraid that he might lose me. And he was probably right, angry as I was. So Nicholas got right to the point. "Man is different from every other creature here on earth. God wanted man to be closer to him. Not the same, but closer. So God gave each of us a conscience, so we would know the difference between good and evil. And God urged us to choose good and avoid evil."

As Nicholas paused for a moment, I interrupted, "Are you referring to the story of Adam and Eve?"

Nicholas acknowledged the question and continued without a pause. "The story of Adam and Eve in the Garden of Eden gives a very graphic description of man facing the choice between good and evil and choosing evil. But just to be clear, Hans, the importance of this story lies in the message. The story relates in vivid terms the message that when given a choice, man chose evil."

I noted Nicholas continued to refer to "the story" and it made me uneasy. "Don't you believe the story of Adam and Eve?"

Nicholas looked at me. "Remember, Hans, much of the history of mankind was first told orally from generation to generation, by word of mouth. And that's the way it was told and retold over the centuries. In preserving the message over all these generations, it was useful to relay the story in a form that created a picture in the hearer's mind. Conceptual terms might shift in meaning. They might not carry the message well and surely would be less forceful. Certainly a compelling story, rich in detail, is more likely to keep the message intact."

I waited, and Nicholas continued. "In this case, the concept that was transmitted is that man was given a choice between good and evil, and man chose evil. That is what we learn from the story of Adam and Eve, the serpent, the tree, and the apple. The basic message presented in unequivocal terms."

Nicholas paused a moment. Meanwhile, I was thoughtful and vaguely uneasy. "So you don't believe in Adam and Eve?"

Nicholas too was thoughtful as he responded, "The message is this. When given the choice, man chose evil. And he would be accountable. This is essential to the subsequent story of salvation. If you find Adam and Eve help you to capture this message with clarity, then they are serving you well, just as they have done from the very beginning. But don't let the details of the story of Adam and Eve distract you from the message that they convey."

I was definitely going to take my time to think this over, but meanwhile, I had a question more important to me. "So what happened when man chose evil?"

Nicholas was solemn. "That changed everything. Man began with a life of happiness, which is described as the Garden of Eden. And man had eternal life, eternal happiness. Then, after choosing evil, man found his life was filled with all the effects of evil, including famine, disease, disaster, war, and many more evils. And ultimately for man, there was death and, during his lifetime, the shadow of death."

I thought for a moment and then asked, "What do you mean by death? Doesn't everybody die at some time or another?"

Nicholas agreed. "Everyone dies, leaves this world. But this death is more than that. This is death in its worst sense. In leaving life on earth, one would face eternal emptiness, loneliness, blackness. Compare that to eternal life, full and overflowing, bright and beautiful, happier than we can ever imagine."

I gave Nicholas a questioning look, a look of doubt. "But how do we know what happens after we die?"

Nicholas was reassuring. "You're right. We don't have a clear picture of heaven or hell, but we do know something about each of them. And what I have just described will at least give you some way of comparing eternal death to eternal life."

I was still puzzled. "With that choice wouldn't man choose to do good? To have eternal life?"

Nicholas nodded and gave a rueful smile. "The sad thing is, man chose evil because it sounded too tempting. And from the time of that original choice, man with his free will continues to make the wrong choice over and over again. We do the wrong thing many times a day. Everyone does."

It seemed to me he painted too harsh a picture, and I questioned Nicholas. "Are we really all that bad?"

Nicholas wasn't moved by my plea. He just nodded and added, "An evil choice is not only doing things we know we shouldn't. Evil also means not doing things we know we should. There are so many ways that we hurt each other. Added to that, we often fail to do things that would help those around us and bring happiness and support. We fail to reach out a helping hand to someone who is hurting."

Nicholas was pretty forceful in pointing out how bad things were, or so it seemed to me. "Nicholas, this is a pretty harsh picture of man," I said, hoping he would soften it.

Nicholas suspected where I was going, and he was quick to respond. "Look around you at all the horrible things that are happening in this world. And when I look at myself, try as I might to do good, I still have memories that haunt me, a conscience that troubles me. It occurs whenever I take a long, hard look at the past."

I guess I was beginning to recognize the amount of evil in this world, the evil that surrounds us, because I started to think about myself and examine my conscience. Nicholas must have noticed the introspective look on my face, because he had a gentle manner as he continued. "When I was younger, your age, it didn't feel quite so bad. Yet there were things I did that I wish I hadn't done. And I know there were opportunities to do good, to help someone, that I let pass by. Often I would regret it, feel bad about it. And sometimes I would have an uneasy feeling that sooner or later I would be accountable."

I grew somber. Somehow the world that God created seemed unfair, and I asked somewhat sharply, "Why did God do this? Why did he set things up this way?"

Nicholas placed a hand gently on my forearm, urging me to be patient. "It all had to do with God lifting man to the level where he had a choice. After that, there was the need for man to live with the results of his choices. He needed to be accountable."

I couldn't see the reason that we lived with evil and all the effects of evil. So I objected with some force. "But I don't understand."

Nicholas nodded in agreement. "You're not alone, Hans. There's much that I don't understand either. I don't understand this world, our universe, life, death, eternity. I don't understand these. How can I expect to understand God? But before you despair, there is a brighter side. When we look for answers, we are reassured in the Bible that now we see through a glass darkly, but eventually we will see face-to-face. Eventually, we will have all the answers. Meanwhile, we know that God is good; he's on our side."

I was thoughtful, but remained unsettled. "So then, did God give man a way out of this?"

At this point, Nicholas smiled. "Of course, he did. He made a bargain with man. It was a promise. He put it much like this: 'Although you chose to do evil, if you change your ways and do good from this time forward, I will give you eternal life.' Doing good meant that I would love God with all my heart and with all my soul and with all my mind and that

I would love my neighbor as myself. That was the bargain. You can call it covenant or testament, or you can think of it as God's promise. He made the promise clear: If you lead a perfect life here on earth, you will be rewarded with eternal life."

I was uneasy about this bargain. "That sounds too difficult. I can't imagine anyone being able to be that good and then do good all the time."

Nicholas nodded, "You're right. That's a huge challenge. No one could do it. But I have to say, the people kept on trying. They would resolve to do good, but then they would start to drift. And soon they would be far from God."

I knew they were likely to fail, but still I hoped they'd find a way to do what God required of them. Sensing the difficulty in all this, I looked at Nicholas. "Did God help them? In any way?"

Nicholas responded promptly. "Yes, he did. God sent prophets to point out how far the people had strayed. They would encourage people to come back to God, to follow his ways. And often the people would do it. But then, in time, they would fall away again, going their own way, paying no attention to God. Over the centuries, it became clear that man was not going to be able to keep his side of the bargain. So, to give them hope, some of the prophets added a further message. They let the people know that in time God would send someone to save them. The prophets called him the Messiah, the sent one. He was also referred to as the Christ, the one anointed to be their king, to lead them."

I felt a glimmer of hope and held on to it. "So did God do it? Did he send someone to save them?"

Nicholas gently touched my arm, urging me to be patient. "First God gave them plenty of opportunities, time for them to see if they could do it on their own. Thousands of years. But time showed they could never meet their side of the bargain."

"But why did God wait so long?" I asked. "Why didn't he send someone to save them sooner?"

Nicholas looked thoughtful. "I believe God gave man all this time so that eventually man would see that on his own he could never earn eternal life. Time enough for it to be clear to man that he could not save himself from the punishment he deserved for his sins. Time enough for people to realize that on their own it was hopeless."

"So when did God decide the time had come to send someone to save them?" I was looking for a happier ending to this story.

Nicholas smiled. "The Bible says 'in the fullness of time' God sent a Savior. It's a quaint term, but it seems just right to me. No logical explanation, just the sense that in God's eyes man had been given all the time in the world, and now the time for a Savior had come."

"So how did God do this? How did he save us?" I asked.

Nicholas replied quietly, "God sent his own Son into the world to pay the price for our sins. Jesus, the Messiah, the Christ. His Son died on the cross, taking on himself the punishment we deserve. This is love for us beyond anything we can imagine. This is God on our side."

There it is, I thought. *God is truly on our side, taking on himself the accountability for all we have done wrong.* I was beginning to believe that he is on our side in everything that happens in life.

For a moment I was lost in thought until Nicholas started to talk quietly of other things. After a few minutes, I noticed he was turning to leave, so I reached out with some urgency and put a hand on his arm. "You still haven't told me about Zechariah's prophecy."

Nicholas nodded and smiled. "No, but we're getting there. Now comes the good part." Then, with a few words of farewell, he headed off to class.

CHAPTER THREE

We Are Forgiven

I was looking forward to hearing what Nicholas had to say about Zechariah's prophecy. But now all I can think about is Lenchen. She gets sick so easily and so often. And it takes her so long to get well again. Actually, she never seems to get over it completely. Today she looks tired, and her little face is pale. While joining us for dinner, she still wears a nightgown drawn snug around her neck to keep her warm.

Yet Lenchen looks mischievous as she smiles at me from across the table. You can never tell whether she is up to something or just inviting me to join her in some game, making it up as we go along. As I look at her now, my smile gives clear evidence that I am on her side, wanting to join her in whatever she is up to. Then, filled with concern, I shake my head to tell her that I don't think this is a good time for any games. She just raises an eyebrow and keeps on smiling. I suppose

I can expect something from her later on today, or maybe tomorrow. Because in any case, she never gives up.

Meanwhile, from my father's end of the table, a question lingered for a moment in the air. I couldn't tell where it came from, but there was a note of hesitation in the voice that asked, which suggested to me that it was from one of the younger students. The question was thought-provoking, or so it seemed to me. How could Christ's death save everyone?

I didn't hear the answer, so I wandered up to my father's end of the table after dinner was over. My father had already left, but there was a small group of students engaged in vigorous debate. I recognized Christopher, a student who had recently joined our household, standing in the middle. I assumed that he had been the one who asked the question, and the discussion around him readily confirmed that. I don't know Christopher well, but I could see he was holding his own in the debate.

Nicholas, standing close inside the circle, had been deep in thought for some time before joining in. Since Nicholas is one of the older students, we all listened closely when he started to speak. "Well, let's go back to where God took things into his own hands. Because man could not save himself by living up to his side of the bargain, God sent his Son to take on the punishment for the sins of all people."

Christopher remained thoughtful, questioning. "But how could he do that?" Nicholas reflected for a moment. Then he smiled, the words coming easily for him now. "It was because of the new bargain God made with man. I can imagine God telling man, 'Since you cannot save yourself, I will accept the death of my own Son as payment for all your sins. By dying on the cross, he will save each of you from the eternal death that you deserve. He will be your Savior. That's my new bargain. This is my promise.' We know it as the New Testament."

Nicholas paused, gathering his thoughts. "By sending his own Son, God felt it was a sacrifice of such great intensity that he would accept it as payment for the punishment that each man, every man deserved. Just think if you were sending your own son, someone you loved so dearly, to die. And to die in such a cruel fashion. So it's not hard to understand that God would say that his death would be sufficient punishment to pay for all the sins of every man."

Another student joined in. "Because he is the Son of God, that means he is God as well. Why did he also have to be man?"

Nicholas nodded, acknowledging the question. "As a man, Christ suffered on the cross with the same agony that you and I would feel if we were nailed onto a tree to die. All the intense pain and suffering that you and I would feel. He was not half God and half man; he was both fully God and fully man. He suffered and died as a man, just like every man he was saving. Just try to imagine a death like that. And he did it for each of us. For you and me. The Bible is very clear that he died for all."

The students were quiet now, waiting for Nicholas to continue. For a moment he looked at them and then stated again with emphasis. "Each of us can truly say, 'God's Son died for me. He paid for all my sins.' We don't have to worry that when we die we will be punished. He is our Savior because he saved us from the punishment we should have received.

He is our Redeemer because he paid the price with his life; he redeemed us."

Thoughtful now, most of the students turned to go, walking off in groups of two or three, while I was left alone with Nicholas and Christopher. I was glad they stayed, because I still had questions. "Please, Nicholas, why did Jesus spend all this time on earth if he really came just to die on the cross?"

Nicholas responded promptly. "He used the time to preach to the people, so that large numbers of people would come to realize that he was the Son of God. And yet, during his ministry, he kept a careful balance. He knew that if he acknowledged outright that he was the Son of God, he would be put to death immediately for blasphemy."

I could see the difficulty. And I could also see how dangerous it was. "Why did he need to gather all these people? Why was it important that they would know he was the Messiah?"

Nicholas was patient. "If Jesus was put to death before the people knew he was the Messiah, they would be left in darkness. They wouldn't know that it was the Son of God who was put to death. They wouldn't know that their sins were forgiven. They wouldn't know that in dying he had earned for them eternal life. They would know that a man had been punished and crucified, but nothing more. It would mean little or nothing to most of them. They would continue on in darkness, not knowing they had been saved."

Christopher and I looked at Nicholas, ready to hear more, so he continued. "Jesus wanted people to spread the good news after his death. People who believed in him would keep the message of salvation alive and would help to carry it forward from generation to generation. So during his ministry, Jesus was gathering people who would do just that, people who believed in him and many more who had listened to him, or at least heard of him. After his death, the disciples proclaimed the good news of salvation, and there were huge numbers of people who believed and helped spread the word. And in fact, that's why we have a church today and find people in countries everywhere who have heard that through Christ their sins are forgiven, who realize that they have eternal life."

I could see that Christopher was intrigued, and I watched him join in. "How did Jesus let people know he was the Messiah without actually proclaiming it?"

Nicholas gave us both a reassuring smile as he continued. "Jesus preached with amazing knowledge and insight about God, his Father. He also explained prophecies in the Old Testament that talked about the coming of someone who would save them… the Messiah, the Christ. In addition, Jesus performed miracles, powerful miracles. These miracles showed God's love and mercy. Jesus healed the sick, the blind, the deaf, and the crippled. He even raised some from the dead. These were exactly the kind of miracles people believed the Messiah would do. And as he did these miracles, more and more people believed that he had come from God."

This seemed a pretty dangerous path to me. "Then how did he keep the balance so that he wouldn't be accused of blasphemy too early?"

Nicholas nodded, indicating he understood the danger. "First of all, he consistently called himself the Son of Man, not the Son of God. In fact, when some of those he cured declared he was the Son of God, Jesus told them not to tell anyone. For example, John the Baptist sent disciples to ask

Jesus if he was the Messiah. John the Baptist spent years in the desert preparing people for the coming of the Messiah, and Jesus was grateful to him for all that he had done. Yet, Jesus knew the danger to his ministry if he answered him directly. Instead, he told John's disciples to look at the miracles he had performed, knowing that John the Baptist could easily draw the conclusion from all Jesus had done that he was indeed the Messiah. Still, Jesus did not openly acknowledge it so he could continue to preach and gather ever more people who believed in him."

We both remained thoughtful, and Nicholas continued. "Jesus knew that in the end he would be crucified. That was what he had come for, and he referred to it as 'my hour.' He knew that when his hour had come, the moment when he was condemned for blasphemy, his death would happen promptly. So on some occasions when people encouraged him to do a miracle, Jesus responded, "My hour has not yet come." He didn't want to give the authorities the opportunity to prematurely accuse him of blasphemy. It wasn't time yet. And in that way, he continued to maintain the balance."

I could see another risk, so I said, "What if people took things into their own hands and declared him to be Christ, the King?"

Again. Nicholas nodded. "Actually, that happened. It was on an occasion when Jesus used a very small amount of food to feed a huge crowd. After they ate, the people wanted to make him king. Jesus responded by crossing to the other side of the lake, allowing them time to cool down."

After considering for a moment, I asked Nicholas, "Why did Jesus do any miracles? After all, he knew that if people said he was the Son of God, they could easily get him into trouble with the authorities."

Nicholas responded promptly. "Miracles helped people to know that Jesus was the Messiah. On the surface, as far as most people were concerned, Jesus was just like any other man. It took a lot of convincing for people to see that he was the Son of God. At one point, Jesus told a crowd, 'You just refuse to believe in me unless I do miracles.' So the miracles helped a great deal. Another advantage was that the miracles attracted large crowds to Jesus to listen to his preaching. And in this way, he gathered many more people who believed or were on the verge of believing."

Christopher nodded his agreement and then pressed Nicholas with another question. "Since Jesus knew that he would end up being crucified, he must have dreaded seeing it come closer. Did he ever hesitate during the years when he was preaching and doing miracles?"

Nicholas was prompt. "He knew that he was here on earth to die on a cross, and he dreaded it. But he knew that was his mission, and he was relentless in heading toward that moment. He waited only long enough to gather sufficient believers. In fact, he became openly frustrated on several occasions when people were slow to believe in him. One time when people showed a lack of faith, he said to them, 'How long must I put up with you people who refuse to have faith?' He knew his path led to the cross, and even though he dreaded it, he was eager to get there."

I was beginning to like Christopher. He asked questions that intrigued me. Meanwhile, I was lost in thought, considering the difficulties Jesus faced during the years of his ministry. In a way, I could understand the eagerness Christ felt to get to the final event of his ministry, the cross, and it prompted me to say, "So when did Jesus announce himself as the Messiah?"

Nicholas answered, carefully taking things step by step. "Near the end of his ministry, he acknowledged to his close disciples that he was the Messiah, the Son of God. But he told them not to tell anyone. Then, when he had gathered enough people to his side, he knew his hour had come. At that point, he turned and made his way toward the cross."

We waited for Nicholas to continue. "He went to Jerusalem, where a huge crowd of people welcomed him, anxious to hear him. Each day they gathered to hear what he had to say. At the same time, he talked a great deal with his disciples in private to prepare them for what was to come. On the night when he knew he was going to be betrayed, he gathered his disciples together for one last meal. He talked with them, giving them comfort and encouragement, because he knew they would be frightened, devastated when they saw him arrested and then crucified. Although he dreaded what lay ahead for him, he kept his focus on them with words like these, 'Peace I leave with you, my peace I give to you. Do not let your hearts be troubled, and do not let them be afraid.' These are words he said to help them, and these are words he also says to us."

Christopher and I were quiet now, waiting for Nicholas to continue, so he went on. "After that, it was all over in less than one day. Late that night he was betrayed to the authorities. During the night, Jesus readily acknowledged to them that he was the Son of God, the Christ. Immediately, he was condemned for blasphemy. By early morning, the authorities convinced the Roman governor that Jesus should be crucified. A few hours later he was nailed to the cross. And by mid-afternoon, he was dead."

Puzzled, I asked, "But where was the crowd that welcomed him to Jerusalem? Why didn't they save him?"

Nicholas responded promptly, "They were likely unaware until it was too late. This all happened during the night. And in the early hours of the morning, there were others gathered who wished him dead."

He paused and then went on, "Jesus always knew what was in store and what it would be like. So after his last supper with the disciples, he went into the garden to prepare himself and to pray. And here you can sense what it meant to Jesus, who was totally man, as well as the Son of God. He had come willingly to this point, and yet, as a man, he dreaded it. He prayed that there might be another way. He prayed this repeatedly but ended each prayer with, 'Not my will, but thine be done.' He prayed so intensely that sweat, like drops of blood, fell from his forehead. But when he had finished praying, he was ready to face what was going to happen, and he walked right up to the man who would betray him."

Christopher broke in. "And it just kept getting worse. They arrested him and took him to the authorities. There they hit him and spat on him. When they had condemned him, they took him to the Romans, where the soldiers flogged him and beat him. Then he was nailed to the cross, where he hung in incredible pain, while his body inched slowly toward death. He felt so isolated, so completely alone. In his despair, Jesus said, 'My God, my God, why have you forsaken me?'"

Nicholas listened quietly to Christopher and then added, "The prophet Isaiah, who lived many centuries before Jesus, described the suffering that Jesus would endure, his words charged with emotion. 'He was despised and rejected of men, a man of sorrow and acquainted with grief.'"

Nicholas looked at us. "If you have had something really terrible happen in your life, sorrow of a kind that grabs at your throat and tears at your chest, then you understand what this means. And in that case, you too can say in what is actually a broad understatement, 'I am acquainted with grief.' And if, for you, the grief won't go away, you too can say, 'I am a man of sorrow.' Words so simple, yet words that capture a relentless grief. And Christ knows exactly how you feel. he understands your grief. Isaiah says, 'He has borne our grief and carried our sorrows.'"

Christopher and I didn't move, so Nicholas continued. "Isaiah knew that Christ was doing this in order to earn our salvation. So Isaiah continued, 'He was wounded for our transgressions and crushed for our sins. On him was laid the punishment of us all. And by his stripes we are healed.'"

Christopher and I listened quietly, and then Nicholas broke the silence. "In all of history, this was the most important moment for each of us. You and I were saved, and so was everyone in the world. And it happened on a dark afternoon with Jesus hanging on the cross. And now, as a result, each of us has eternal life."

I looked at Christopher, but he remained quiet. I wanted to hear more, so I turned to Nicholas. "What happened then?"

"Jesus rose from the dead, assuring his disciples that he truly was the Son of God," Nicholas replied. "On Easter morning, the tomb was empty. Then Jesus visited his disciples, talked with them, and ate with them. After that, he went to heaven. As he left them, he asked them to tell everyone the good news. Spread the gospel to the ends of the earth! Let people everywhere know that they have been saved! And as the word spread, you can imagine the excitement. Today you would hear church bells, cathedral bells, ringing loud to celebrate the good news that we have been saved and are at peace. And each of us would say to our neighbor, 'Did you hear the good news? Just listen!'"

We stood quietly for a moment. Then Christopher broke the silence, "But do you have to believe in order to be saved?"

Nicholas was firm in his answer. "The Bible says he died for all. It doesn't say he died just for believers."

Now I joined Christopher as we challenged him, "But there are passages that say that people who don't believe in him are damned."

Nicholas looked at us, his expression kind but unruffled. "Some ancient authorities omit some of these verses, suggesting they may have been added later. It may have been that good men, with good motives, felt that by adding these words, they would encourage people to believe so that they would know they had been saved."

Christopher and I were together now as we objected. "But how do you pick and choose? How do you know which passages to believe?"

Nicholas gave a reassuring nod. "Look, the central story of salvation is clear. It is stated over and over in the Bible that Christ died for all. The sins of the whole world have been forgiven. That message is so clear and repeated so often that I question things that do not fit in, that are not consistent with that message."

Christopher and I were both thoughtful now, and I have to admit I was puzzled. In any case, I wanted to understand it better. "So it doesn't matter whether you believe or not? You're saved in any case?"

Nicholas was unshaken. "In fact, you are saved in any case. Because it's not up to you… it's up to God. When Christ died on the cross, he saved everyone, every single person. That happened when he was crucified, and it doesn't depend on whether you believe it. With his death, Christ has given each of us eternal life. But here is what believing does, the beautiful thing about believing…those who believe have eternal life starting now. That is the joy of believing. Jesus said, 'I came that they might have life, and have it abundantly.'"

As we listened, Nicholas continued. "When we know our sins are forgiven, we no longer need to fear that we will be punished. At that moment, we walk out of darkness into the light. And when the time comes that I leave this world and walk through death's door into eternity, I can be totally unafraid. The blessing for me here on earth is that I feel at peace. I'm at peace with God, and I'm at peace with myself."

As we watched Nicholas, he smiled broadly. "So now we come back to Zechariah's prophecy. He knew that God had sent a savior, soon to be born of Mary. So Zechariah told us what this would mean. 'By the tender mercy of our God, the dawn from on high will break upon us, to give light to those who sit in darkness and in the shadow of death, to guide our feet into the way of peace.'"

Nicholas paused for a moment, searching for words. Then

he added, "Zechariah is giving us the news that Christ would come to save us. Our sins forgiven, we would live in peace. This is what it means to walk out of the darkness, into the light."

Christopher and I were both thoughtful. Then Christopher began slowly, "You think of all the prophecies so long ago that pointed to Christ. And now we have the books of the New Testament that tell us what Christ has done. You would think that everyone would believe."

I quite agreed with Christopher, but Nicholas replied, "It's not that simple. Actually, there are many reasons people find it hard to believe."

He was ready to continue, but by now I wanted the chance to check once more on Lenchen and see how she was doing. "Nicholas, I need to go," I started to say.

Without waiting for me to continue, Nicholas nodded, understanding immediately.

Actually, Nicholas loves Lenchen almost as much as I do. But I was really surprised when I looked at Christopher. The thought of Lenchen brought a change. He looked downcast; you could almost say worried. It amazes me how Lenchen finds a way into everyone's heart.

I like Christopher. More than that, I feel we are kindred spirits, although I can't explain why. One thing I do know, Christopher's concern for Lenchen has already assured me that we will be friends. We talked for a few minutes, and then we said goodbye. I watched Christopher disappear through the doorway, his blonde hair such a contrast to the dark, curly hair that often helps me identify Nicholas, even from a distance.

When I reached Lenchen, she had already gone to bed early and now was sound asleep. Her face was pale against the pillow, causing my concern for her to border on anxiety. But as I watched her, I sensed her breathing was quieter than when I had looked in on her the night before. I hoped with all my heart that it was a sign that she was on her way to getting better. As I sat quietly by her bedside, my anxiety gradually lessened, and I felt more at peace. I began to realize that she no longer had episodes where she struggled for breath—episodes that had worried me ever since she fell ill. I never tired of looking at her face, gathering strength of my own based on a belief that her strength was returning as well.

Later that night, asleep, I dreamt about Christ's suffering. I think the emotion I felt during my discussion with Nicholas and Christopher still lingered. When Jesus said to his Father, "Not my will, but thine be done," I wondered what thoughts were going through his mind. Then, slowly, a picture formed, and I imagined what those thoughts might be.

"Not my will, but thine be done." The phrase is so small and concise, yet it says so much more. There is life and death in this phrase. When Jesus says, "Not my will," his flesh is speaking. "I don't want to die. I don't want it to happen. I dread it so much that I am breaking out in sweat like drops of blood. I have come to the garden to pray, because without praying, I don't know if I could go through with it. I'm young. I'm full of life. I don't want to die."

And yet, with courage and resolution, Jesus says, "Thy will be done. If it takes me dying to save each of you, I will do it. If it will be that awful death of hanging on the cross until life is wrenched out of me, I will do it. If that is the only way to save each of you, if that is what it takes, I will do it."

I could see him turning to his disciples. "Come now; it's time to go." He was ready to face the misery, the abuse, and the humiliation. Then, he's on the cross. He's wretched, exhausted, and still the agony goes on. It's relentless. Consumed with suffering, he is still concerned about us. As he feels his life squeezed out of him, he assures the man on the cross next to him that all will be well. As the pain peaks, as death comes faster now, I dream that he says, "Father, please forgive them. They are so lost. Forgive them, they don't know what they are doing. Here, let me die for them. But please forgive them." Then in my dream his Father says, "Yes, I do forgive them. You have taken their punishment on yourself. Their sins are forgiven. Yes, I do forgive them."

Jesus bows his head, failing quickly now, his final words: "It is finished." Thy will be done. Death has arrived. But for the rest of us, it is the beginning. The penalty is paid, our sins are forgiven. Our sins are not merely overlooked, but they are completely washed away. This is God's gift to us.

Then, in my dream, I see the glory of the resurrection. Risen from the dead, Jesus appears to his disciples, speaking with them and encouraging them. As he does, we are assured that Christ, no longer dead, lives eternally. He is our Savior, our Redeemer, our friend. My dream, at first so dark and gloomy, is now a happy dream, a glorious dream. Christ is risen. Jesus is constantly by my side. And in my dream, I join the disciples as they raise the cry, "He is risen!"

And all around there is a resounding echo: "He is risen indeed!"

I awoke, still in the quiet of the night. I had been so deep in thought, so troubled, when I went to bed. But now I'm relaxed, once again assured of being at peace with God. I am content.

With a sense of quiet happiness, my mind drifts slowly to where Lenchen lies sleeping. The longer I watch her, the more frequently a curious thought floats through my mind. It seems to me that although she is deep in sleep, at some even deeper level of consciousness she is planning some mischief, looking for a chance to outdo me. And blessings on her if she does, if only it means that she is inching back to good health. I am already looking forward to tomorrow.

CHAPTER FOUR

Grace, a Gift from God

With a sparkle in her eyes, Lenchen walked slowly up to me as I sat quietly in the garden the next morning, getting ready for the day. She tried to master the look of a young adult, but she was far too happy. Instead, she exuded the open carefree happiness that lights a child's face. Lenchen loves to give the impression she is older than me, treating me as someone not quite capable of caring for myself, someone who needs her guidance, a youth who needs her adult supervision. She tries to look demure and innocent, but the mischief in her eyes betrays her.

The sun was bright, warming us and telling us that summer would be coming soon. It was a great time for a walk, yet I was uneasy about activity that might tire Lenchen so early in her recovery. Before the morning was over, my worry for her was replaced by quiet admiration. Her courage and her spirit inspired me. She gave a charming performance of the heroine in one of our favorite plays, while I took the role of the villain. No matter that she was cheered while I earned scornful looks from the little group that gathered to watch. It was an enthusiastic audience, consisting of our brothers Martin and Paul and our sister Margaretha. Martin, at seven, was the oldest and was also the most vocal. Margaretha, at four, was the youngest and was clearly the most in awe.

Our little play ended happily, the heroine prevailing, the villain in chains. The audience clearly enjoyed the outcome, clapping and cheering. Lenchen was their heroine in life, as well as on the stage. I too admired her as she bowed to the crowd, tired yet triumphant. I encouraged her to rest, and I was happy and relieved as Lenchen walked toward the house with her brothers and sister in tow.

Meanwhile, I viewed the disorder that resulted from our play. My father had made it clear that our front lawn should provide an appropriate setting for the many colleagues and friends who visited. I was eager to meet his expectations and hoped I could do it quickly enough to be in time for dinner. It was unusual for anyone to be late. Our home, while full of love, was well regulated, and meals were on time. Perhaps it was the only way to serve our extended family and the students who shared our table.

As I worked, I had a momentary view of my mother in the kitchen window, and then heard her call to me. I must be the only one missing from the table. My mother's voice usually conveyed a message of love when she talked with us, but this time her tone was firm. Then she disappeared without waiting for a reply.

Shortly thereafter, Aunt Lena appeared in the kitchen

doorway and slowly made her way along the path to me. With a welcoming sweep of her arm, she brought me to her side. A moment later we were walking toward the house. Aunt Lena had a hand on my shoulder and a gentle smile on her face. I was relieved she had made the decision for me, and I would finish the lawn later. I am always more comfortable with Aunt Lena by my side, and so it happened as well just now. I was feeling rather better about the whole affair until I walked into the kitchen, where everyone was seated, and each gave me a questioning glance. A few of the students gave me a brief but welcoming smile. My father, on the other hand, gave me a longer and more thoughtful look. Quite serious, in fact, and accompanied by a slight frown.

And yet my embarrassment subsided quickly as I glanced across the table at Lenchen, her face radiant with friendliness. She can charm me in a moment, as she did right now. My love for Lenchen knows no bounds, as does her love for me.

Fortunately, the conversation at the kitchen table was brisk, and I was able to dissolve into the background. Attention was focused on my father, who was discussing faith, a favorite topic of his. I caught the last words of a Bible verse he was quoting: "that you may come to believe that Jesus is the Messiah, the Son of God, and that through believing you may have life in his name." There was no mention of saving people from damnation. Instead, there was the promise of life. I was intrigued and set out to find Nicholas as soon as dinner was over.

I drew him into a quiet room adjacent to the kitchen, one of my favorite places for us to talk. I could sense that the discussion at the kitchen table still captivated Nicholas.

Without waiting for a question, he began to talk. "Like your father said, faith brings us eternal life right now. We already have our salvation. Christ saved each of us when he died on the cross. The sacrifice earned redemption for everyone, everywhere. But faith allows us to know that this is so. Without faith, we don't know we have been saved. We live in darkness. It is faith that brings us out of darkness. Faith brings us eternal life now."

Christopher must have overheard us, because as he walked in, he began to speak, showing the excitement that carried over from the kitchen table. "Your father emphasized that faith is a living, active thing. It was a surprise for me to realize that faith is not a set of beliefs, but a force that changes who I am."

This was getting interesting, and I asked, "What do you mean by a force?"

Once again, Nicholas took up the discussion. "Let me set the stage. When Jesus was alive, people were looking for, hoping for, the coming of the Kingdom of God. In those days, an earthly kingdom was not defined by borders on a map or on the ground. A kingdom was the area that reached out as far as the king had influence or, in some cases, had absolute power. When people asked about the Kingdom of God, Jesus said the Kingdom of God is among you, within you. God's power as king has always been there, for the Kingdom of God comes without our prayer. But when Jesus was among them, preaching and doing miracles, people could feel his power within them."

Nicholas paused for a moment and then continued. "After his death, when Jesus was preparing to leave his disciples, he assured them, 'But you will receive power when the Holy Spirit has come upon you.' This is the power that comes to us each time we encounter God in the Bible or the sacraments, or when we come to him in prayer. This is the power that brings us faith. When Jesus was here on earth, it was the power of his preaching that instilled faith in those who listened. Now, for us, it is the Holy Spirit who instills faith, if only we come with an open mind. Because the Holy Spirit is known by what he does, we may refer to the Holy Spirit as the power of God in our lives. Just as we know Christ by what he did, as our Savior."

Christopher was following closely, and now he added, "Through this power, our faith becomes a force in our lives. If we believe, then we will have the blessing which this gift brings, the blessing of living in peace, knowing that we are saved. If we believe our sins are forgiven, then eternal life starts now. That is what faith does for us."

Nicholas nodded. "The force of faith in our lives is evident in so many ways. Along with faith comes the power to resist temptation, the power to be strong, the power to have courage, the power to endure. I know that God is always by my side. Faith helps me to see it, to feel it."

I spent a moment thinking about this, taking it in. Then another thought crossed my mind, and I looked at Nicholas. "Is that really the only way to get faith?"

Nicholas smiled and nodded. "Yes it is. Let me give you an example. On one occasion, two young men who wished to know Jesus and understand his message approached him and asked, 'Where are you staying?' Jesus replied, 'Come and see.' That is the message to each of us who wish to know Jesus:

'Come and see.' For us, it is, 'Come to where you hear the gospel.' The Holy Spirit will bring faith if we just come and see. So there is your answer. Come with an open mind, and you will find faith."

As I listened, Christopher joined in. "Being open-minded may sound easy, but coming with an open mind is really the difficult part. Christ tells us we must come like children. You can imagine a child with his parents, accepting with an open mind what his parents have to say. As adults, that's not a picture we want of ourselves. We pride ourselves with being open-minded, but at the same time, we want anything of importance to be supported by evidence, by logic."

Nicholas agreed. "In a sense, I have not only asked that we as adults put logic aside, but when I say we must come as children, I have really challenged the very basis of who we are…the view we have of ourselves as adults. I'm a mature person, I'm logical, and I'm certainly not a child. Yet, I am told that when I listen to the gospel, I cannot rely on logic and I cannot weigh the evidence. I cannot analyze it as an adult, but instead, I must approach it as a child. And this I cannot do without a battle. The thought is outrageous, and it is a huge challenge to overcome that. It is an attack on who I am. No wonder that the inner conflict is so intense and the battle is only won when I listen to the gospel with an open mind. Then God takes over, and faith begins to grow."

I was thoughtful before nodding slightly and then admitting openly, "I know it's still a problem for me. A child talks about Jesus, a person who lived and died while saving us. I feel more comfortable talking about Christ and the role he played in obtaining our salvation. We are saying the same thing, but I find I feel more comfortable when I talk of concepts rather than consider the person, the man who actually lived and died. In fact, when talking to adults, I rarely speak of Jesus. And at times like that, I remind myself to look at Jesus through the eyes of a child and think of the person and how as a man he died for me."

There was a slight pause, and then Nicholas continued. "I've had people ask me how to find faith or how to regain faith that has been lost. If I suggest to them that they approach the gospel with the open mind of a child, they glance at me with a kind but dismissive look. In fact, those present may even feel a moment of embarrassment. And then they glance away, seeking to return the conversation to a more adult level, hoping to discuss this in theological terms. And I understand. As an adult, the last thing I want to do is look childish or to be a child who accepts things on blind faith."

Christopher nodded. "And yet, a child is not blind. He is just not burdened with the attitudes and mind-sets that we accumulate as we mature. As an adult, I pride myself in my ability to analyze the data and draw conclusions based on some element of proof. And if proof is not available, I want convincing facts that lead to a logical conclusion. We pride ourselves on making decisions that are based on the evidence, yet logic will not lead us to believing the good news of the gospel. Philosophy will not get us there. Deep theological discussions will not get us there. Perhaps that is why Christ says so often that we must become like children."

I was uneasy. So I asked, "Do you mean you must accept it without thought?"

Nicholas shrugged. "As long as you realize that you cannot

think yourself into faith, then thoughtfulness is fine. There is much about religion and our relationship to God that is enhanced by our thoughtfulness. It is said that when Mary was told that she would be the mother of Jesus, she pondered things. But it is important to note that she did not let her thoughtfulness get in the way of seeing a miracle and accepting the news by faith."

I knew my faith wasn't that strong, and it worried me. "Sometimes I feel my faith is strong. Yet, why does it feel so weak at other times?"

Nicholas smiled. "It happens to all of us. There are so many things that can distract us. Jesus talked about this to his disciples. I would have thought that the things that would most distract us would be the love of money or power or the lure of pleasure. In fact, these may distract me from my faith, but I was surprised that Jesus headed the list with 'the cares of this world'… our worries, our anxieties. And then I realize how much of my day is crowded with things that cause me concern and preoccupy me. Certainly, I need to address them, but the challenge for me is to assure they don't squeeze out my faith. And it is critical that I meet that challenge. In fact, I find that keeping my priorities straight is a task that I struggle with every day."

I considered the effort it has always taken me to keep my faith strong, and I asked, "I believe my sins are forgiven, and I know that for me eternal life starts now. So then, why is it important that I keep my faith strong? What is the value of prayer or reading or going to church?"

Christopher considered me for a moment. I think he knew what a struggle this was for me. He was gentle as he replied,

"If I lose my focus on faith, daily cares and concerns start to fill my day. My faith gets weak, and doubt and indifference creep in. I no longer have the same certainty that my sins are forgiven or the same conviction that I have been saved from punishment. I can feel myself losing my sense of peace. But then I pray for God to help me, and gradually, I become aware again of how closely God has me by his side. As I put things in perspective, faith assumes its rightful place. I feel my heart and soul at peace. I have this profound joy of knowing I'm at peace with God and with myself. Yet every day it takes renewed effort. I have the same challenge and the same reward."

I indicated that I understood. Then another thought struck me. "Since it all depends on faith, wouldn't it be great if God performed a miracle that was so powerful that everyone had to believe?"

Nicholas smiled, understanding why it sounded so good to me. It was a question he had heard often from his friends. "In Christ's time, miracles certainly helped people to believe, but they were not intended to be so forceful that people had to believe. With all the miracles that he did, some believed he was the Messiah, and many did not. Today we have the whole story of salvation laid out for us in the Bible. So now, in our time, miracles might well be so convincing that people were forced to believe. God wanted man to have a choice, not be overwhelmed."

My eyes lit up. "Well, if it's all a matter of faith, certainly we should get credit if we believe."

This time Christopher responded. "Forgiveness, salvation, eternal life, and even faith are all God's works. None of it is our work. We cannot reach out and grasp faith. In fact, we cannot claim any credit for finding faith. Thankfully, when we listen and read with an open mind, God does the rest."

I was puzzled. "But certainly we should at least get credit for coming with an open mind."

Nicholas smiled. "I'm sorry, Hans, but if you give a starving man food, you don't give him credit for opening his mouth. The same is true with food for the soul. It's no credit to me if I come with an open mind. My salvation is a free gift from God, given freely to me from beginning to end… completely free."

I was lost in thought for a moment and then asked, "Really? Entirely free?"

Christopher assured me, "The grace of God means exactly that. Grace is not what God gives us, but how he gives it… freely, as a gift. Salvation comes at no cost to us. And it comes with no strings attached. So every time you read or hear the word *grace*, think: *It's free.*"

When I looked chagrined, Nicholas added, "I know it's hard to admit that it's all in God's hands. I like to feel I have some control, play at least a little part in my salvation." He paused for a second and smiled before adding, "Here I am, striving to put myself right with God, while meanwhile, God has already done that for me."

I could see his point. Yet, I pushed further. "What is there about being right with God? Why do I want to put myself right with God?"

Nicholas looked at me closely, his eyes probing mine. "Because I face death, sooner or later." He paused, considering for a moment. Then he continued. "It is difficult, I believe, for someone who does not believe to be confident and at ease, totally at peace when facing death. Yet, being at peace is huge. To know that any sin, no matter how big, is already forgiven by God, to know that and feel that in your soul brings peace that is truly a life changer. Having faith means knowing that now. It means having eternal life now. It means knowing that death is only a transition into the heavenly world where eternal life will continue. Christ said he wants us to have life and have it more abundantly. To me, that means living with joy and being at peace at the end of the day. This is the peace that faith brings."

I had one last thought. "Salvation is a free gift from God, this I know. I cannot contribute to my salvation, this I understand. So now, at this point, is there nothing we can do?"

Nicholas's face broadened into a smile. "Actually, we can do a lot, but none of it for credit."

I waited for a moment and then asked, "So please tell me what I can do."

"I will," Nicholas replied and threw a friendly arm around my shoulder.

CHAPTER FIVE

We Say Thank You

I could see the quiet relief in Aunt Lena's eyes as she glanced down at Lenchen, happy that the color was returning to her cheeks. I noticed how close she sat to Lenchen, in a comfortable, protective way. As I glanced at the two of them from time to time, I grew happier and more relaxed. Sitting together at the kitchen table, sharing our food, I had a growing sense that Lenchen was safe with us. I was beginning to think our concerns for her health could be put to rest. I loved the sparkle in her eyes, her spirit of adventure, and her determination to win.

Craning my neck slightly, I began to follow the conversation at my father's end of the table. Then, with a casual glance across the table, I noticed Aunt Lena had a smile that reached wide across her face, a smile that clearly demonstrated the love she had for Lenchen, and one that suggested something special was about to take place. Aunt Lena was holding a locket in her hand, showing it to Lenchen. It was a locket I had often seen Aunt Lena wear, one that obviously meant a great deal to her. Watching the two, my face broke into a look of wonder and happiness at the thought that Aunt Lena was offering to Lenchen something that was so dear to her. At the same time, I could see Lenchen was reluctant, uneasy at the thought of accepting such a precious gift.

Then I saw my mother turn quietly to Lenchen and speak to her in a voice both tender and firm. "This is a moment when you need to say, 'Thank you.' It may seem to you that it is far too great a gift, much more than you deserve. And you are right. It may feel to you that you should do something to earn it, but there is nothing you could ever do. There is no way to earn it. And so you struggle to know how to respond. Yet, all you need to do is look at your Aunt Lena. You can see that she is giving this freely to you. It is truly a gift…her gift to you." My mother paused while Lenchen nodded. Then she continued. "You will make her very happy by simply saying, 'Thank you.' For she will know that thank you comes from the love you have for her deep within your heart."

My mother was right, of course. Lenchen's face was radiant as she turned to her aunt, expressing her thanks. At the same time, Aunt Lena's face filled with equal happiness as she looked down at Lenchen. A gift of great value was met with a thank you from the heart. It was as it should be.

I continued to think about my mother's advice. Saying thank you was the right thing to do. It was such a simple thing, yet it had not come easily to Lenchen. She needed to be reminded. I wondered why this was so, and soon I was lost in thought. Then, listening to my father speak about our salvation, it came suddenly to me that I needed to be reminded as well.

When God had given his son to die on the cross for people who were sinners, it was the ultimate act of love. With salvation came eternal life, peace with God, and peace within myself. It was a gift so great that it could never be repaid. So I too should do exactly as my mother had said. I should simply say, "Thank you." But now I was faced with a dilemma, and I looked for help. By that, I mean I looked for Nicholas.

I found both Nicholas and Christopher walking in the courtyard. I waited for a pause in their conversation and then touched Nicholas's arm. He turned with a smile, as did Christopher. So I asked them both, "How do I say thank you to God?"

Christopher looked at Nicholas, then back at me, gathering his thoughts. "We thank God by showing him that we love him. The more thankful I feel, the more I feel my love for God. But that feeling of love for him can easily be lost as my attention wanders. I am so often distracted by cares and worries and by everything else that the world has to offer. Yet if I stop for a moment to think, I am reminded of the blind man who came to Jesus, pleading with him, 'Let me regain my sight.' I come to God with the same plea many times: 'Let me regain my sight.' And with those words, I focus again on what God has done for me. Then love for God is natural and comes easily."

Nicholas joined in. "And, of course, the best way to show our love for God is to love our neighbor. Love is an action word, much more than a warm feeling. A man asked Jesus,

'Who is my neighbor?' Jesus told him a story that reminds us of what it means to love your neighbor.

Nicholas continued, "The story Jesus told was about a Samaritan who found a stranger lying by the road, beaten by robbers, and fairly well ignored by others passing by. The Good Samaritan took this poor fellow to a place of safety, where he recovered from his wounds at the Samaritan's expense. Jesus wondered if the man could tell him, 'Who was the neighbor to this poor fellow, of all the people who passed by?' The man replied, 'The one who showed him mercy.' Jesus did not say, 'Yes, you are right.' Instead, he said, 'Go and do likewise.' That's an important lesson to us. Love is an action word. Love is doing. We love our neighbor best by doing things for him."

I understood the call to action to do things. But, still, I wondered how. So I said, "I wish I lived near a hospital, or maybe near some poor people."

Nicholas smiled but shook his head. "You remember Mary's response to the angel, 'Here I am.' They are three little words, but they say so much. And we can say them to ourselves now. *Here*, in my present circumstances, here in this place, I will find opportunities to love my neighbor. *I*, not someone else. I cannot point to others and tell myself that it would be easier for them. Here I *am*, present tense, and I cannot put it off. It may sound easier to do things later, some other time but here I am. So, look around you. There is no lack of opportunity and no lack of examples of people who helped, who cared, who showed mercy. 'Go and do likewise.'"

Christopher was eager to join in. "Here's another way to be a good neighbor. Don't judge! It's just that simple. Don't judge! Yet, it's surprising how difficult that is. It's almost like I can't help myself. I find myself constantly judging. I pray God for help. Jesus said it over and over again as he talked to the people. He urged them, he begged them, 'Don't judge.' It's true that Jesus was openly angry with some in those days because they were opposing him and making it hard for people to believe in him. He also spoke out vehemently against every kind of sin. But he was remarkably kind to the sinner."

Nicholas continued. "There were those who wanted to test him, so they brought a woman who had been caught in adultery, which was a capital offense in those days. They pointed out that the law prescribed death by stoning and asked Jesus what he thought. It would seem to be a simple, straightforward case. But he answered famously, 'Let him without sin cast the first stone.' When they gradually walked away, he was left with the woman. Jesus looked at her and said, 'Where are those who condemned you?' She said, 'They all left.' Jesus said to her, 'Neither do I condemn you.' Then, condemning the sin, he told her to change the way she was living. I can imagine he said it firmly but kindly. And he left the rest of us with a powerful lesson about not judging each other."

Nicholas looked at each of us and said, "And here's another thing about loving my neighbor. I need to forgive my neighbor like I forgive myself. There are things that I do, or even parts of my personality, that I wish I could change. In fact, I work on changing them. But until I do, and that may be never, I bear with them. In the same way, I need to bear with my neighbor, forgive him like I forgive myself. Sometimes when I find it difficult to forgive, I have to remind myself how much God forgave me."

Christopher was ever more thoughtful as he joined in. "There are so many ways to love your neighbor, Hans. Here's something to think about, something that may help. Many of the things that happen around me, that I am tempted to react to, have nothing to do with me. A friend looks at me without a smile, or even snaps at me, and I feel hurt or am tempted to respond in kind. Instead I say, 'It's not about me.' And almost all the time it's true. The person was having a bad day, was distracted, or had a problem of his own. When I tell myself, 'It's not about me,' I avoid making things worse. I give my friend space, while I keep my own happiness. On occasion, it may have to do with me. But that can wait until my friend is ready to talk, and we can deal with it then. You don't need to think about in the meantime. And I am surprised how often it was not about me, how often it never comes up and things were quietly resolved all because I had taught myself to say, 'It's not about me.'"

I was hesitant as I glanced at Christopher. "It may be easy to say, but I don't know if I could convince myself that it's true."

Christopher nodded. "In the beginning, you may find it hard to believe, but gradually as you say, 'It's not about me,' and find it to be true, it will become easier. And in time you will find that you are saying it with conviction, recognizing truly that it is not about you. And at that point, you realize all the trouble you have saved…for yourself and for others."

We each thought about it for a moment. Then Nicholas broke into a smile as he looked at Christopher and me. "Here is something equally important about love. We know we should love our neighbors as ourselves. But here is something that we should also consider. We should be as kind to ourselves as we are to our neighbors. Sometimes in our efforts to help those around us, we find that we are pushing ourselves too hard, actually neglecting our own needs. It may even get to the point that important relationships are becoming frayed. We may find that we are putting ourselves through more than we would ever ask of another. Loving my neighbors means loving everyone, even myself. We should love our neighbors as we do ourselves, and love ourselves as we do our neighbors."

Christopher and I smiled. We understood, and we agreed. As we did, Nicholas continued. "Remember that there is no limit to love. God loves each of us with as much love as he loves all of us. When I love one person, it does not mean I love someone else less. I love each one with all my heart. Some things in life are limited, others are not. For instance, my time is limited. I may spend more time with one and spend less time with another. Yet that does not equate with love. No matter how much we love, our love is never limited, never depleted. There are no bounds to love. So it is for God's love. So it is for me. And so it is for each of us, for everyone."

Nicholas was more thoughtful now, talking from the heart. "There is a special blessing that comes back to us when we do something out of love to our neighbor. It comes across so powerfully to me when I think of Christ on the cross. It is important to remember, Hans, that although Christ was fully God, at the same time he was fully human. He was as human as you and me. He felt all the pain and anguish that you and I would feel. When Christ was dying on the cross, he was in agony, wretched and alone. He felt deserted by God.

Even though his pain was worse than anything we can ever imagine, at that moment he took the opportunity to show his love for the man on the cross next to him. He said the most comforting words of all, 'Today you will be with me in paradise.' And with these words, Christ in his humanity reassured himself as well that he too would be 'in paradise today.' When he felt at his worst, while he was in his greatest agony, as a man he asked God to forgive those who were crucifying him. 'Father, forgive them for they know not what they do.' And in focusing on forgiving them, in focusing on saving them, he found reassurance in the recognition that only through his death on the cross could they be forgiven."

After a small pause, Nicholas continued. "This lesson from Christ has been powerful for me. There are times in my life when I have felt miserable. They were bitter times, times when I felt alone. At times I was hurting, sometimes grieving. At times like these I have felt the most comfort by thinking of others who might be sharing that grief or others who also had pain or who felt alone. If I talked to them, or wrote to them, giving them words of comfort as best I could, I found my own grief or pain or loneliness subsided. We were in this together. I realized that my words to them came back to me. And I felt more at peace."

I thought of the many ways love fills our lives. When I love my neighbor, I say thank you to God. When I love my neighbor, I often find that I am equally blessed. Then Christopher touched on one more way that my love for another can be a blessing to me, and he said, "As I think about someone I truly love, I am struck by the thought that to love another person… to have that opportunity…is the greatest joy in the world.

Certainly, being loved brings us intense happiness. But the greatest gift you can give me is the opportunity to love you."

That evening, as I sat in my room, taking a moment before getting ready for bed, I thought about love. There were so many that I loved...my father, my mother, my family, my friends. I thought about my love for Lenchen. I knew she loved me dearly. And it warmed my heart to think of that. Yet the greatest gift Lenchen has given me is the opportunity to love her.

As I thought of love, I couldn't help be reminded how much I was going to miss my family when I headed off to the university the very next day. My father had picked a school for me that was some miles away. My mother did her part by reassuring me that my education was important, that the university my father had chosen would be the best for me, and that leaving home to go to school was all a part of growing up.

Young as I was, I could see the wisdom in their plans for me. And yet the thought of leaving home weighed on me. Thankfully, Nicholas and Christopher were full of encouragement. Still, despite their enthusiasm, from time to time my courage would falter and fail me. And in those moments, what helped me most was the pride in Lenchen's eyes as she talked of my departure for the university. I expected to be homesick, but her pride in me kindled my pride and strengthened my determination to do well. And so, after one more night's sleep at home, I would be heading off to the university tomorrow. And with that thought, I felt my life stretch out before me.

CHAPTER SIX

We Are Inspired

Sitting at the kitchen table, I have the strange idea that I need to introduce myself again to those around me. Fifteen years old and home for a short vacation from the university, I am sitting straight and tall, hoping that those around me will recognize how mature I've become. But then, on the other hand, I'd be surprised if they even see me. Everyone looks at Lenchen, who is the one your eyes go to naturally. She's adorable, charming, innocent, and full of fun. I'm thoughtful, careful, respectful, and almost invisible.

There is much about Lenchen that brings us joy. But there is heartache as well. She's been sick again. She coughs, she's tired. It happens so often that I'm beginning to be afraid for her. I know I can't show it. Maybe she's afraid as well, even though she doesn't show it. Her cheerful smile, her arched eyebrow, and her mischievous grin still cheer me. But her face is thinner and has lost its color.

Dear Lenchen, what shall I do with you? My heart breaks for you. All the more because you show no sign of giving up. And more still, because I can do nothing to protect you.

So I sit across the table. I match her grin with one of my own, and I let her know with my eyes that any mischief she is up to will find me a willing partner. I'll be there. You can be sure we'll have a grand time.

As I sit, my mind drifts. Then slowly I let it focus on a determined debate at my father's end of the table. In a spirited fashion, the talk revolves around the question: "How is the Bible inspired?" I've often wondered, so I didn't waste a minute when dinner was over. As my father rose, the students, of course, rose with him. Then gradually we all got up to leave.

I gave Lenchen a smile to let her know that I'd be looking for her soon. Meanwhile, I caught Nicholas' eye and invited him with a nod to follow me into the parlor next door. I was hoping that Christopher would join us, and I was happy when I saw both of them come in. One, tall and slender with dark curly hair, the other shorter, solid build, with straight blond hair, the two of them make quite a contrast. Yet, in other ways, they are very much alike…compatible, congenial, friendly.

As we gathered, Nicholas began without waiting for a question. "When you talk of inspiration, you are bound to get a heated discussion. You could hear how strong the opinions are. Some believe that every word in the Bible comes from God. They believe, in effect, that the Holy Spirit dictated every word as the authors wrote each of the books. Verbatim."

As Nicholas paused, I broke in. "Is it true?"

Nicholas nodded thoughtfully. "It certainly is true for

them. Others believe that the Holy Spirit gave the authors the message and let them put it in their own words."

I was puzzled. "But how do you know which of them is true?"

Nicholas shook his head thoughtfully. "Well, for each of these groups, that is the truth as they see it."

I felt lost. "So, Nicholas, what do you believe? How is the Bible inspired?"

Nicholas was reassuring. "I am convinced the Bible is inspired by the way that it inspires me. I feel my faith growing. It's the Holy Spirit, the power of God, working through the Bible to instill faith and to strengthen faith." There was a pause, and then he continued. "The Bible is inspired in that the power of God is in these pages. But it does not lie quietly. The power, the force, comes through these pages to the one who reads, who listens, who comes to the Bible with an open mind." There was another pause, then he added, "Look, Hans, inspiration is not so much a matter of what the Bible is as what the Bible does. The Bible is inspired in that the Bible inspires us."

I was still searching. "But how can you prove that it's inspired?"

Nicholas continued. "It's not a matter of proof. There is no proof. Remember, inspiration is an action word. So I can judge it by its actions. I can see the people who have been inspired by the Bible. And when I read the Bible, I feel inspired as well. When I'm inspired, it doesn't mean my spirits are lifted. It means my whole person is changed."

I thought about that. "What do you mean 'changed?'"

Nicholas saw I was perplexed, and he smiled. "When I

read the Bible and when I hear the good news that every one of my sins has been forgiven, I can scarcely believe it. But as I continue to read and to listen, my faith increases. That's what inspiration does, that's how the Bible inspires me. Convinced that I have been saved, I am at peace. And with a heart that is full of thanks, I love God for what he has done. And the best way of thanking God is loving my neighbor. That is what inspiration does to me. That's the power of inspiration, the power to change my person. That's inspiration in action."

Looking at Nicholas, I could see how strongly he believed. I could sense the power that was driving him. But I still had questions. "I can see what you mean about the power of inspiration. But, Nicholas, when I read the Bible, there are some passages that really speak to me and others that I have trouble with. Some are hard to understand and some seem to relate only to those times. How do you pick and choose?"

Before Nicholas could answer, Christopher broke in, eager to respond. "The Bible is written by a great many authors and told from different viewpoints, and understandably, some passages can seem confusing. Yet the story of salvation is very clear. Here, start with this. We are sinners. Long ago man chose to sin, and we continue to sin many times every day. In accordance with the initial bargain God made with man, we deserve to be punished with eternal death. So, on our own, we lost our chance for eternal life. But God came to our rescue. God took it all on himself. He sent his Son to die for us, and by dying on the cross, Christ paid in full the penalty for all our sins, every single one. He did it once… for all…for every person, past, present, and future. He died for the sins of the whole world. He died for all. The sins of each of us have been forgiven. And with our sins forgiven, we have eternal life. This is the story of our salvation, Hans. When you read the Bible, keep this story in mind. You will come across passages that you can feel strengthen you and build your faith. These passages inspire you. If you come across other passages that don't build your faith, don't be distracted by them."

I was curious. "You mean some are not inspired?"

Christopher shook his head. "It means they're not inspiring to you. Maybe some of these will become inspiring to you when you know more about them. Perhaps some will never be inspiring to you. But you will find so many that are strengthening to your faith. These are the ones to focus on. You will feel the power of inspiration by what they do to you."

I must have looked rueful, and I could feel it in my voice as I said, "Still, I wish there was something solid."

This time Nicholas broke in with a smile. "There is. The story of our salvation is very solid. It is clear, and it is confirmed over and over again. So when you come to other passages that you may find puzzling, remember what your father said. Truth is not a rock, it's a shining light. I try to keep that in mind. I look at the light of truth from many sides, and then I come back and look at it some more. And so my understanding grows. And my faith grows. And if you do the same, you will see that the central story of our salvation remains clear, solid, unchanged."

I sat quietly for a moment, and I'm sure my face showed signs of my acceptance. Still, the questions did not quit. "The story of salvation is clear. I agree. But then, why do we have four gospel stories? Why not just one? Why wasn't one enough?" I asked.

Nicholas nodded, showing he understood. "There is strength in hearing the same story told from four different viewpoints. These were men, just like every other man and woman on earth. They were doing their best to describe what was going on around them, describing the man who was central in their lives. Who was he? Where had he come from? What had he done? What effect did he have on the whole world, on everybody who had ever lived, or would ever live? The central story of our salvation is the same, but there is a richness about hearing the story from each of them, from each of their viewpoints."

Nicholas could see we were following him closely, so he continued. "The word *gospel* means 'good news.' The good news, of course, is the story of our salvation. The four evangelists are writing the good news, presenting it as a record that could be conserved for all to see and to hear. Let me describe how each of the evangelists looks to me.

"As Matthew told the good news, he pointed out that the story of our salvation is firmly grounded in the Old Testament. Next comes Mark, who wrote a more condensed version, precise and to the point. Luke's account is beautifully written, providing detail that is not found in the other gospels, yet the basic story of salvation is unchanged. John was one of the twelve disciples, and he felt particularly close to Jesus. John gives a powerful account of Jesus talking to the disciples on the night before his crucifixion, preparing them for his death. Jesus helped his disciples understand the importance of the cross, and he wanted them to have courage and faith even as they saw him die. Here are four people, each coming from a different viewpoint, but each telling the same story of our salvation."

BEYOND ALL EXPECTATION

I was beginning to understand, but I reached out for more. "Do you ever find that the difference in detail among the four raises questions in your mind, makes it more difficult to believe?"

Christopher was ready. "Not as long as the central story stays the same. In fact, sometimes the variation in detail makes it more convincing. It reminds me of any four witnesses giving their versions of an earth-shattering event. Just consider for a moment the accounts of Christ rising from the dead. To understand the impact of that event, we should begin by walking with the disciples as they followed Jesus during his ministry, listening to him preach and seeing his miracles. They could feel the excitement in the crowds grow as more and more people believed that Jesus truly was the Messiah. The disciples could see it more clearly, and they were convinced that Jesus was indeed the Christ, the Son of God, who had come to save his people. But then, in the space of a day, they saw his capture, his crucifixion, and his death. Try to imagine the disciples' reaction. It was devastating. And it was so final. He was dead. Their whole world had turned upside down. The disciples themselves feared for their lives. You can sense the hours going by as the disciples became increasingly despondent, trying to adjust to the horror of their loss."

I didn't say a thing, just stood thinking. Quietly, Christopher continued. "Then, imagine the news comes that he is alive! The disciples running to the tomb, seeing angels, seeing Jesus. Christ is risen! He is the Son of God! Before his death, he told them that he would die to save us all. He told them he would rise again. They realized that all of it was true.

JOHN MARK

And the truth of it changed their lives. Then, much later, you can imagine the disciples as they recounted it, Matthew and John writing it down, some of the disciples telling it later to Mark and Luke. Each was focused on the fact that he had risen. Each was searching his memory for the details. 'Who got there first?' 'Was there one angel at the tomb or two?' 'Was there really an earthquake, or did it just seem like that to me?' It is just as you would expect from those who witnessed a startling, life-changing event. The central story of the resurrection is absolutely clear, and yet the details vary. For me, the difference in detail from each of these witnesses adds to the reality of what they say. It is what I would expect. For me, it makes each account more convincing. And of greatest importance, although the details vary, the central message is the same: He is risen. He is risen indeed."

And so the discussion ended. We didn't have much time to say our goodbyes before Nicholas and Christopher hurried off, heading to the university, hoping to get to their lectures on time. As I stood watching them on their way, I paused to think how freely they shared with me what they had learned from my father and from the Bible.

They were certain to relate my father's views just as he expressed them. Then, at times, they gave me views of their own. I know they took earnestly my father's observation that truth is a shining light to be viewed from many sides. Yet, their views were always based firmly on the scripture.

They did not take issue with the views of others, and there are many. They focused on the essence, the central message of our salvation, which is so clearly related in the Bible. They talked to me of the power it has in their lives, how the scripture inspires each of us, and how we can respond to the good news. They are my friends, and I owe them much.

As they passed from sight, I turned and walked off silently, the thoughts revolving slowly as I sought out Lenchen. I was surprised and happy to find her fast asleep. A nap was likely the medicine she needed most. And I was grateful for the opportunity to be at her bedside. It seemed to me that she was safer when I could see her. And I was happy for the opportunity to sit back and think. At one point, an Old Testament passage drifted through my mind as I considered the story of salvation and the power of inspiration. It is an interesting verse that urges us to make straight the paths of the Lord. Perhaps at times we have made the message complicated and the path crooked. Man has a tendency to do that. And we each have a strong desire to be in control. Yet the central message in scripture is clear and straightforward. Christ saved all of us and paid the penalty for all our sins. He did it once for all, on the cross. Freed from the penalty for our sins, we have eternal life. There is no action we must take. It is a free gift from God. We should not make it complicated or add conditions. As my mother had urged Lenchen so long ago, there is nothing more to do at a time like this than say, "Thank you."

Sitting quietly at Lenchen's side, I did, in fact, thank God for all he had done for me, for the gift of salvation he had so freely given to me. And as I said thanks to God, my heart felt at peace. I was at peace with myself, and even more, I felt at peace with God. It was a sense of peace beyond anything I had expected. It made me think with gratitude that this is how the Bible inspires us. When we hear the message of our salvation, we find peace and show love. This is how inspiration changes us.

I was lost in thought when Lenchen stirred ever so slightly. I watched her carefully for a moment and then felt reassured as she settled back into a deep sleep. My mind carried me back to the happy times we'd had together earlier in the day.

Lenchen, I do my best to cheer you. And even when you're ill, you do so much to cheer me. We are each other's keeper.

CHAPTER SEVEN

Interactions with God

As I took my place at the kitchen table, Lenchen looked up at me through carefully narrowed eyes designed to imply that she had a plan in mind. Something to taunt me, hopefully even to embarrass me, but most of all to express the bond we have between us. Far from feeling wary, I felt cautious happiness and relief. Lenchen is showing sure signs that she is battling her way back to health. In Lenchen's case, that means close to health. She never seems to get totally well, back to her old self. The stronger she gets, the more she pretends that her illness is behind her. But a little cough betrays her. I adore the way she looks at me as though she has the upper hand. If her health could be measured by her spirit, she would be well indeed.

Happily, I have reinforcements. Aunt Lena loves Lenchen as much as I do. Although I'm away so much now, Aunt Lena keeps a watchful eye. And best of all, Aunt Lena is as spirited as Lenchen. She brings an exuberance that does not allow any sense of worry or unhappiness to surround Lenchen. The two of them are quite a pair. They are convincing in their determination to get the better of this illness. And from deep in my heart, I hope they are right.

As the conversation grew louder at my father's end of the table, I began to pay attention. They were talking about baptism and the Lord's Supper, the sacraments. Discussion grew into debate, which came to a climax as my father hammered the table firmly with his fist, driving home his point. My father guides every discussion, even the most heated debate, never in anger, but certainly with authority. Meanwhile, the students are writing furiously in their notebooks. I suspect that our table talk shapes opinions more than the lectures at the university. I'm beginning to understand these discussions better now, but I still look forward to hearing what Nicholas and Christopher have to say.

Before we rose to leave the table, I glanced at Lenchen and signaled her with a very carefully manufactured frown. It was designed to inform her that I am on to her and that she will not get the best of me. She can expect to see me later. I'm looking forward to seeing what she has in mind. Each time I join her in any of these escapades, I begin with a determination to beat her at her own game. Yet, I rarely win, even though I continue to show her that I'm putting in my best effort to thwart her. My prize is seeing the joy in her eyes when she comes out ahead.

When Nicholas and Christopher joined me in the parlor, I had my question ready. "If faith comes to us through the word, of what use are the sacraments?"

Nicholas was ready. It was clear he had been thinking about it as well. "We talk about the word and the sacraments as though they are separate, but actually, in each sacrament, both are present. There is an act, and there are words that are spoken. Take baptism, for instance. The washing signifies that all my sins, past, present and future, have been washed away. Forgiveness happened long ago when Christ died on the cross for all of us, for the whole world. My baptism makes it personal. My baptism focuses on me, and the words emphasize that the forgiveness of sins applies to me. And then throughout my life, my baptism reminds me that I live as a child of God, my sins washed away, forgiven."

I was cautious. "But how does baptism do this?"

Christopher was eager to join in. "Remember what your father taught us. Without the word of God, baptism is just simple water. The words spoken bring power to the baptism. Whenever I encounter the gospel, or whenever I hear the good news that I have been saved, there is power in these words, and my faith is increased. The combination of word and action in baptism makes it an even more powerful experience, a personal interaction with God. Those present during the baptism play a very important role as well. If parents and sponsors are present, the words addressed to them during the baptism ask them to make a commitment to bring up the child with the sure knowledge of God's salvation. If the baptism is performed in the presence of a congregation, then all those gathered express their commitment as well to help the person baptized keep a strong faith in Christ."

I paused for a moment to consider this. Then I pointed out, "But there are so many different ways to baptize."

Christopher nodded. "You're right, Hans. But while there are many forms of baptism, I focus on your father's point that it is the word that accompanies the baptism that makes it a sacrament. The washing is a powerful experience, while the words bring meaning to the baptism. In every form of baptism they work together in bringing faith."

Deep in thought, another question came to mind. "Do you need to be baptized in order to be saved?"

This time Nicholas jumped in. "Clearly not. Our salvation occurred a long time ago. God forgave the sins of the whole world when Christ died for mankind on the cross. It was then that Christ saved us. The thief on the cross met Jesus for the first time when they were being crucified. He said to Jesus, 'Remember me when you come into your kingdom.' And Jesus responded, "Today you will be with me in paradise.' Salvation is for all."

Christopher's face showed his agreement. Then he added, "Even though baptism is not actually necessary, Hans, it is a powerful means of increasing faith. And beyond that, during my baptism, my parents and my sponsors pledged to help guide me, agreed to help me to have a strong faith, and promised to keep me in their prayers. My baptism means everything to me."

There was a momentary pause, and then Nicholas pointed out, "Just like baptism, the Lord's Supper combines the word with a personal experience. And this is how it came about. Remember, during Jesus's ministry he knew it would end with his dying on the cross to save the world, to save each of us, as he paid the penalty for our sins. As the time came close, Jesus knew his hour had come, and he had one last supper with his disciples to prepare them for his death and to encourage their faith."

Nicholas could see that I was watching him closely, so he continued. "Jesus emphasized that it was his death that brought forgiveness for everyone, and for each of them individually. Then he provided a powerful experience for each of the disciples. He took a loaf of bread, blessed it, then broke it and gave a piece to each, while saying, 'Take this and eat it. This is my body given for you for the forgiveness of your sins.' Then he took a cup of wine, blessed it, and said, 'Drink from this, each of you. This cup of wine is my blood poured out for you.' This is the new covenant, the new bargain between God and man."

While Nicholas paused, Christopher picked up where he left off. "As the disciples ate the bread and drank the wine, the message was clear and powerful. Jesus was dying so that man might live. And it was personal. As they ate a piece of bread and drank a sip of wine, each one could understand so clearly, *This sacrifice is for me. This new covenant with God is my new covenant.* Salvation is for all mankind, but in this sacrament it becomes personal. As I eat and drink, the focus is on me. Salvation is for me. My sins have been forgiven, and I have been given eternal life."

While I remained thoughtful, Christopher continued. "When Jesus told his disciples to eat the bread and drink the wine, he said 'Do this in remembrance of me.' Always remember what God has done for you. Remember that your sins have been forgiven. Remember that you have eternal life. You can see how powerfully this message comes to us in the Lord's Supper."

From their voices as they talked about the Lord's Supper, I could sense the power of this sacrament in their lives. I thought about this for a moment, and then I asked, "So this is a reminder?"

Nicholas gave me a reassuring smile as he continued. "A reminder and much more. It is an experience—an encounter. As I eat the bread and drink the wine, I come face-to-face with what Jesus did for me. I can hear him as he says to his disciples, 'This is my body; this is my blood.' The encounter is that personal." He paused, then continued. "And as the words sink in, I have renewed faith that my sins have been forgiven and that I have eternal life. And more than that, I am reminded that I have eternal life now. Knowing this, I am at peace. This is what the Lord's Supper does for each of us."

Later that evening, as I was wandering through the garden, I spied Lenchen sitting quietly on a bench, hunched over ever so slightly. I was worried at first, but as I approached, I could see she was comfortably snuggled in a blanket.

She was watching the sunset in a happy but thoughtful mood. The bright yellow of the sunset was beginning to pale, while the clouds deep in the west were taking on the faintest shades of pink. As we watched, the pink slowly matured, gradually becoming a deep, vivid red. Dusk continued to fall as the sun slowly dipped below the horizon. Then, suddenly, the sky once again brightened as the sunset filled the sky with a grand display, a flare of brilliant red. It was glorious, as radiant as sunsets tend to be. Then it too faded as nightfall approached.

Watching the sunset, I am often thoughtful, sometimes wistful. A sunset is so beautiful as it evolves, but the changes carry with them the inevitability of dusk. I didn't break the silence as I took a seat next to Lenchen.

She looked at me for a moment and then continued to follow the sunset, watching pensively as the clouds began to gray. "Where does the sun go, actually?" she asked softly, even as she continued to watch the evening slowly become a darkening shade of gray.

There's no question she's getting better, I thought with relief. Her skin, so pale recently, was beginning to take on a slight, but very welcoming touch of color. And yet the question gave me pause. She asked it with a steady voice, to be sure. And yet her face remained thoughtful, even somber.

"Why, Lenchen," I said, assuming the authority of a young scholar, "it is hurrying along as fast as can be through the darkness so it will be ready for the dawn."

Then she turned slowly to me, her eyes pensive, her voice still steady. "Do you ever worry that it might stay away? Never make it to the dawn?"

"Never," I said. "I never worry. The sun always comes back. It has for thousands of years. It never fails."

"But if it did …" she said, her voice trailing into a question.

"Well, then," I responded with a quiet laugh meant to reassure her. "Why, then we would be the first to view this miracle." I paused while I considered her through a gentle smile, then added, "But I doubt we'll get the chance. The sun is too determined to show itself again. It doesn't want to become a miracle by its absence. Maybe it's too proud. It loves to hail the dawn and then light up the day."

This time Lenchen gave a quiet laugh. "I'm glad. The sun is my best friend." She looked at me with her famous imitation of a scornful glance. "Not like some people, who go off and take too long in coming back."

Although her tone was playful, I felt myself grow more thoughtful. "I know," I said, then paused. "It doesn't seem right. But then, it has to be if I am going to become a scholar, maybe even a professor."

Her eyes were wistful, but her manner was steady and thoughtful, without the slightest reproach. "I want you to stay just as you are."

"But just think of the sun," I replied. "It has to go away so it can come back to us again. If it didn't go away, we would never have the joy of seeing a new dawn."

This time her face softened, showing just the hint of a smile. "I like it that way. I like to see you coming through the door. Even when you're away I can picture that."

With that, I actually lifted her up, blanket and all, and carried her to the house, her arms and legs trailing as we went. She was perfectly able to walk, but her illness gave me the excuse to carry her and the chance to hold her gently for a few minutes, the bond between us as tight as ever.

"And now, off to bed," I said with my newfound authority. Lenchen grinned, indicating that in her mind I had no authority at all. But she was happy to go to bed.

"And tomorrow morning," I said, "the sun will greet you with a happy smile and maybe nod a gentle reminder to you that it never plans to alter its routine."

She smiled. "I know." She paused and then gave me a superior look. With a commanding voice, she said, "And don't you ever either." She yawned, and then added, "Always come back. Just stay as steady as the sun."

She turned to the steps that would take her to her bed, then glanced back at me and arched her eyebrow as though to say, "I've got my eye on you."

And as she slipped out of sight, I thought as well, my mood so much like hers. *Lenchen, I too have got my eye on you. I depend on you to be my lodestone, my bedrock, the cornerstone that keeps me founded on things that make my life secure, the love of family, the joy of kinship, the happy sense of needing each other, and being needed.*

We have a bond that will endure a lifetime and beyond. Even when I'm at school, she's never far away. Never will be, never can be. And with that happy thought, I slowly headed toward my room and to the book that awaited me. After just a few pages of my book, I found I welcomed sleep, and it welcomed me. As I drifted off, I relished the security of the household and the love that surrounded me.

Yet a couple hours later, in the quiet of the night, I found myself awake. I had slept well, but now, in the solitude of my bed, I thought about the discussion earlier in the day.

We interact with God in so many ways. Reading the Bible, listening to the gospel…in each encounter we find our faith increased. In our prayers we have a more personal interaction. While each of these encounters draws us closer to God, the water in baptism and the bread and wine in the Lord's Supper impress on us even more powerfully this personal interaction with God. We see, we feel, we taste, and we actually have an experience in which the love of God and his salvation is inescapably ours. And for each of us individually, this becomes personal. This is my interaction with God. He gives me of his own, and I am his.

CHAPTER EIGHT

The Church Spreads the Good News

As I look around the kitchen table and see all the faces I love, I am filled with nostalgia. Tomorrow I leave to go back to the university, and I am already feeling a twinge of homesickness. But when I see Lenchen, happiness prevails. The color is back in her cheeks. An occasional cough is the only reminder of her battle back to health these past months.

Lenchen doesn't want to see me leave. But she cannot suppress a grin as she recalls yesterday's success. Well, departure is still a day away and seeing her gloat reminds me that there is time yet for more encounters. There are schemes to be plotted and battles to be won and lost.

But before I can engage in today's adventure, I look forward to talking with Nicholas. And maybe with luck, Christopher will join us as well. He always brings a light and eager spirit to our discussions. Today I have questions about the church, of all things. It seems like such an ordinary subject, but I heard spirited debate at my father's end of the table while I was distracted, thinking about my last day at home before returning to school.

When at last I caught Nicholas' eye, he smiled and wandered in my direction, talking to others as he came. And happily, I could see Christopher approaching from another direction. Standing there waiting, I was considering in an absent-minded way how many church bodies there are and all the different ways of worshipping. But as we walked together into the parlor, a sudden thought came to the surface. "Tell me, Nicholas, since my sins were forgiven when Christ died on the cross, what does the church do? How can it help me?"

Nicholas thought for a moment, and then he replied with a smile. "It's easier to understand when you think of how the church first started. As Christ prepared to leave his disciples after his crucifixion and resurrection, he told them to spread the good news of salvation to the ends of the earth. Tell everyone we have been saved from the penalty for our sins. Spread the good news that Christ has earned eternal life for each of us. That's what Christ asks of us. Just tell the news, tell everyone."

I understood what Nicholas was saying, but still I was puzzled. "Since everyone has had their sins forgiven, everyone is saved, why is it important to go to the ends of the earth to tell them?"

Christopher was eager to join in, and he replied, "Remember, Hans, our mission is to bring light to people in darkness, not to save them from hell."

I was surprised, and I'm sure I showed it, but Christopher went right on. "The Bible says Christ died for all. By saving us from our sins, he earned eternal life for each of us, for all of us. Now, if I've never heard this, or if I don't believe that my sins are forgiven, I remain in darkness. It's what the Bible means by living in the shadow of death. But if I believe my sins are forgiven, then eternal life starts now. I realize that death is just a doorway along our pathway of life, with no fear or worry or slightest doubt about the life of happiness beyond the door. My faith has brought me out of the darkness. I no longer live in the shadow of death."

I understood what Christopher said, but I looked for reassurance. The question still nagged at the back of my mind. "Are you sure you don't have to believe in order to be saved?"

Nicholas replied, "God gives us salvation as a free gift. It is all by the grace of God, entirely free. But there is a tendency to put ourselves in charge. And we say, 'If you don't believe, you won't get to heaven.' It's up to you. Yet the message of salvation is clear. Christ died for the sins of the whole world. God's gift of salvation is his gift to each of us."

I considered this and then asked, "So believing doesn't change anything?"

Christopher smiled. "It doesn't change the story of salvation, but it changes what you do with it."

I looked puzzled. But Nicholas gave me a reassuring glance, "You are bringing light to people in darkness. You are bringing good news, telling the story of our salvation. It's all positive. Not a mention of damnation, not a mention of hell. Just tell the good news that Christ has earned eternal life for each of us!"

I think my face showed I understood. And yet, I had great doubts about an earlier point. "You don't believe in hell, Nicholas? And you either, Christopher? You don't believe in hell?"

Nicholas looked reassuring. "This is the hell I believe in, Hans. To be in hell is eternal death. This is what we learned in the Old Testament. People had lost eternal life because they chose evil over good. And given a second chance, they found that they could not earn eternal life because they could not keep God's law perfectly. So that meant we were condemned to eternal death. It meant spending our time on earth believing, fearing, that we will be punished for our sins. That is the hell I believe in."

Still, I was curious. "But what about the fiery flames of hell?"

Nicholas nodded. "I have always been impressed with the ability of the Hebrew language to express things with powerful imagery. For instance, instead of using a Greek concept like sympathy, the Hebrew language speaks of 'the bowels of compassion.' Instead of God regarding us with love and kindness, we hear that 'God makes his face to shine upon us.' So in those early days, I can understand using vivid imagery to describe the punishment we deserved. I can understand warning of the fiery flames of hell to portray the most horrible punishment that one could imagine. I can understand using a picture that would be clear to everyone and would help them understand how horrible a punishment they deserved."

Christopher joined in. "The fiery flames of hell created a picture that could be easily understood, one that would carry the message from generation to generation. A picture that would not fade over time. A picture that is accurate in the way it describes the most horrible punishment conceivable. Accurate in the same way as the bowels of compassion describes sympathy."

I was thoughtful. "What about heaven?"

Christopher replied, "We don't know much about heaven, but I do know that we will be happy. Everyone's idea of happiness varies. Just try to imagine some of the happiest times in your life. Heaven will be happier than any of these. It will be happier than anything you can imagine."

Although I was happy about heaven for those I love, I was troubled by another thought. "I can't believe that bad people will end up in heaven. I mean, really bad people."

Nicholas's response was prompt. "Well, Hans, first of all, God reminds us that we all fail in so many ways that we should not judge others. We do things we shouldn't and fail to do the things we should. But I know what you mean about really evil people. And for these, Christ says, 'Leave judgment to God.' Perhaps it would be easier if we could convince ourselves to judge the sin and leave it to God to judge the sinner."

I was dubious, and at that point Christopher joined in. "Think about the thief on the cross. He was so evil that the authorities condemned him to death. Not only death, but death by crucifixion. And even more, the thief agreed that he had been so bad that he deserved to be crucified. Yet when he turned to Jesus on the neighboring cross and said, 'Remember me when you come into your kingdom,' the response from Jesus was, 'Today you will be with me in paradise.' A clear reminder to each of us of how important it is to leave judgment to God."

Still, an earlier question of mine kept coming back, and I wanted them to tell me more. "Since the sins of each of us have already been forgiven, is it even worthwhile going out to faraway places to tell people about salvation? Or, as you say, to save them from darkness?"

Nicholas put his arm around my shoulder, "Just consider this, Hans. If you are in darkness, you are left with the sense that you will have to pay for your sins, that you will be accountable. You are left facing death with uncertainty or with fear. When you deal with hardship or tragedy, you are left without knowing there is someone who cares, someone who loves you, someone who has you by the hand. You are left alone with your grief, your heartache, your pain. You may feel unloved, without hope. When you face difficult choices, you do not know that God brings courage and strength to those who seek it. Eventually, when you get to heaven, you will know that God has saved you and given you eternal life. But here on earth you are left in darkness."

I looked thoughtful, and Nicholas continued. "In the Old Testament, a prophet spoke of the future coming of Christ. 'The people walking in darkness have seen a great light. On those living in the land of the shadow of death a light has dawned.' People in darkness may fear that death leads to nothing more than emptiness, or, even worse, to accountability. For these people, death casts a long, dark shadow, a shadow filled with doubt, fear, and dread. By reaching out to these people, we turn that dark shadow into the bright light of knowing Christ has saved us and that we each have eternal life. When you know you have been saved, then you realize that your life has a happy ending. For someone to live and die in peace is one of the greatest gifts that person could ever have. So, Hans, we still have the same urgency in our mission work."

Nicholas smiled. "Just remember, Hans, we don't bring people to Christ by making them fear hell but by offering them the joy of knowing that they have eternal life."

I understood, but still, I wondered how the church fit into my life, and without a pause, I put the question to both of them. "Just consider me, for instance. What more can the church do for me since I already believe?"

Christopher was prompt in his response. "Things are going well for you now, Hans. But you know how cares and distractions so often creep in. You get busy with things. And then, when you need it most, your faith seems distant, God feels far away. It's good to know that when you ask God to strengthen your faith, the church can help."

"But how?" I asked.

Christopher was quick to reply. "We hear God's word, and we pray. When we receive the sacrament, we come face-to-face with God's love for us, his forgiveness. We often find ourselves asking God for forgiveness, but how much better to be reminded in church that God has already forgiven our sins. In so many ways, the church helps me keep a focus on God and reminds me that God is always by my side. And so, with faith comes courage and strength to face life's problems."

I nodded quietly as Nicholas joined in. "A prophet in the Old Testament talked about God in this way. 'He gives strength to the weary and increases the power of the weak. Even youths grow tired and weary, and young men stumble and fall; but those who hope in the Lord will renew their strength. They will soar on wings like eagles; they will run and not grow weary, they will walk and not be faint.'"

I was beginning to feel so much better as I thought about the church, but there were questions that lingered. "Why are there so many different branches of the church? Why not just one church?" I asked.

Nicholas considered for a moment. "In a sense, there is just one universal church. In the Apostles' Creed we say we believe in 'the holy Christian church, the communion of saints.' Your father pointed out that 'the communion of saints' is a phrase that defines what is meant by 'the holy Christian church.' And to help us understand that even more clearly, your father noted that the word 'communion' would be more appropriately translated 'community.' So the church is the community of saints."

I looked at him. "Saints? Really? Come on, Nicholas. There are a lot of people in church who do not look like saints to me."

Nicholas grinned, nodding in acknowledgement. "I know what you mean. But look, Hans, we are not saints because of what we do, but because of what Christ has done for us. He paid the penalty for all our sins. Even though we sin daily, the sins are forgiven. So God has, in fact, made us saints."

I must have looked dubious, because Nicholas reached over and touched my forearm in a reassuring way. "Initially, it's hard for each of us to think of ourselves as saints. And certainly we can't be proud, because it was a gift from God. But it emphasizes for us what God has actually done. All of our sins have been forgiven. He's wiped the slate clean. Not in some abstract way, but actually in real life. When he tells me to go and sin no more, he knows, and I know, that I will sin again. Yet, I know that when I fail, that too will be forgiven. So clearly we are saints, and all because of what God has done for us."

After a pause, Nicholas went on. "But within the universal church, there are many different church bodies. Some are based on differences in interpretation. Some differences have to do with how churches try to instill enthusiasm in our worship, to capture again the enthusiasm that we see in the Bible. When Christ was teaching people in the temple during his final days before his crucifixion, the Bible says the people were spellbound. Later, there was great excitement and enthusiasm in the early church as the good news of salvation spread and the church grew. Are we still spellbound today, Hans, when we hear the gospel?"

I could see his point and had to smile. Meanwhile, Nicholas went on. "Churches today want to generate that same enthusiasm. Some do it with inspiring organ and instrumental music, some with choirs and congregational singing. Some churches have colorful ceremony. In some, the enthusiasm is generated by the preacher's style. But among these different church bodies there is much that is the same. At the center, there is the good news that Christ died for our sins and that God has had mercy on us and has granted us eternal life. This message is presented in whichever style the church feels is most effective. And every time we hear that message, the faith of each of us is strengthened."

Nicholas added with a smile as he and Christopher turned to leave, "And so we continue on, caring for each other while we spread the good news to the ends of the earth."

Late that evening I stood in the doorway of the darkened room where Lenchen was sleeping. Her younger sister Margaretha was tucked in close beside her. It was a room full of innocence and fun. I knew I would be leaving for the university long before they would awaken. *Lenchen, you are my lodestone. You keep me focused, alive, following my course.*

Hours later, I woke in the night, lying quietly, warm and comfortable, listening to the night sounds, considering again our discussion of earlier that day. I know that in the early hours of the morning, the darkened miles will pull me slowly away from my home, my family, and my friends. Yet, I knew that just as surely as the miles separate me, the memories of the kitchen table will bring my family and friends back into full view. Lenchen will look at me from across the table with her mischievous smile, and a sense of happiness will well up inside of me, drawing me out of the darkness.

With the dawn, I was on my way back to school. The trip was long. But in fact, the hours helped me in the transition from home to my world of studies. Then, soon after I arrived in the university town, I found that once again I was in the bright light of college life.

Attending lectures, talking at length with fellow students, and reading far into the night made the transition complete. And as I settled in, the days melted into months, studies alternated with short visits home, and so a couple years passed slowly by.

CHAPTER NINE

God Answers Prayers

*A*message from my father arrived early this morning. The message is brief; there are no details. Lenchen is ill. And yet, I know there is more. The message in its brevity tells me it is urgent. As quickly as I can I am on the road. The trip is long, endless, or so it seems. And as my thoughts wander, there is no respite, nothing to keep me from sinking into despair.

At last I am home. And walking into her room, I see my thoughts confirmed. The doctors are worried. There is nothing more they can do, and she is getting worse. Sad eyes brightened when she saw me, while my sad eyes turned to tears.

Lenchen, no matter your battle with illness, you are stronger still than me. Courageous, determined, resolute, you will not let your illness gain the upper hand uncontested.

My mother is close by her bedside. My mother's face is

kind as always, yet with its softness strained with worry, grief. Her love for Lenchen is displayed in her hands as she gently cares for Lenchen, in her voice and in her touch as she gently soothes her, and in her eyes as they trace every detail of Lenchen's face.

I stepped back into the adjacent room, lit only by a few candles and ringed with grief. In a chair nearby me, Margaretha has found comfort on her Aunt Lena's lap. Almost too big now, she hangs on to her perch, and both find comfort in each other's closeness. Margaretha is crying silently, tears running down her cheeks, while Aunt Lena wipes them gently away from time to time. Aunt Lena is known by each of us as a source of strength and happiness, but today the joy is altogether gone. Her strength remains and is a source of strength in turn to each one she encounters.

The boys stand together by a doorway opposite me, each trying to look grown up, while their faces reflect the overwhelming sadness in the room. I can sense they felt it important to be present, yet they stay quietly at the periphery. The doorway seems safest, where they stand tall, their faces devoid of emotion, almost wooden. Then, at times, their faces begin to crumple, tears forming and an inner struggle playing out, until once again their faces become stoic and they resume their silent witness of the tragic scene, the sorrow that surrounds them.

A short time later I walked again through the doorway of Lenchen's room. Now my father is at the bedside, talking quietly to Lenchen, soothing her. Yet as I listen, blow follows blow. As my father talks to Lenchen, I hear him encouraging her not to be afraid, gently urging her to be at peace. With each moment, I grow yet more bitter.

When I stepped back into the doorway and turned to face the adjacent room, there to my relief stood Nicholas, his love for Lenchen clearly on his face, clouded now with worry. Yet, he had a face that also told of peace. And I sensed a source of strength in him as he turned and made his way toward me.

He threw an arm gently over my shoulders, then stood silently watching my father encouraging Lenchen. My bitterness broke through as I turned my head toward Nicholas and said quietly but emphatically, "I don't want to hear about peace! I want her to get well. How can I think of peace if she continues to get worse?" I spoke in a low tone so that my father would not hear and gradually let the words drift into silence.

Nicholas didn't respond immediately and we stood watching Lenchen, both wordless now, but with so many thoughts absently competing with each other. You might almost think we were calm, standing motionless side by side, until you saw how tight the muscles were in our faces, our arms, and our stance. I gradually regained control and continued. "I have been praying constantly for Lenchen to get well. I pray all the time. But it seems to mean nothing. There's no response. What good is prayer if it doesn't work at a time like this?"

Nicholas drew me toward a set of chairs. We sat, and as he looked at me, I noticed his face soften as he responded. "Let's think about prayer, try to understand prayer. Let's think how we should pray. For instance, right now, while I pray for Lenchen's health, I am focused on the hope that she may improve. But what if she gets worse? What if her illness gets the better of her?"

We sat in silence as this dreadful thought took hold. Alternately, I pushed it out of my mind, and just as often, it slowly crept back in, until finally it took hold, and I could not rid myself of the despair that accompanied it. Nicholas slowly roused, his voice incredibly sad and yet a voice of kindness. "We have to consider that all our prayers for Lenchen's health may come to naught. Then what are we left with?"

I did not reply, and a few minutes later Nicholas resumed. "We can consider the possibility that we didn't pray hard enough, often enough. In that case, we will add guilt to our sadness. Guilt along with our despair." Nicholas paused and then said with emphasis, "It would be so wrong to think that we are at fault if Lenchen does not get well."

I turned slowly, thoughtfully toward Nicholas. My eyes, still sad, entertained an element of interest. Nicholas waited and then continued. "Here's another possibility. We could believe our prayers were not answered because God does not care. Yet, he cares so much for each of us that he sent his Son, deliberately sent his Son, to die on the cross to save us from our sins."

I was silent still, yet giving Nicholas my full attention. After a few moments, Nicholas went on. "You may hear some people say in resignation when a loved one dies, 'Obviously, God had other plans for him.' If I thought God would let Lenchen die at age thirteen because this was his plan for her, I would be so bitter. Tell the mother who watches her child dying of starvation that this is God's plan for him. Tell a young wife whose husband is killed in an accident that this was God's plan for them. Tell the mother that, tell the wife that, and then encourage them to love God. They would have nothing to do with such a God. They would hate God."

I was even more thoughtful now, sitting quietly as I watched Nicholas. As he paused, I asked, "So what's the answer?"

Nicholas responded with a kindly smile. "Let's see what Christ tells us about prayer."

I nodded silently in agreement, so Nicholas continued. "Hard as it is to accept, the world is full of evil. That includes disease, terrible accidents, and famine, along with all the evil, hateful things people do to each other and the devastation that occurs from acts of nature. These are the evils that we find around us and sometimes find in our lives. And we cannot pray our way out of these evils. Once we accept that we cannot change these with prayer, then we can consider what God's role is when any of these happen. How we can bring God to our side when we need him so badly."

I waited, looking expectantly. In the meantime, Christopher had joined us, and now he spoke up, "When I am faced with a difficult situation and I pray to God for help, he always answers me." He clearly had my attention, so he continued, his voice kind and firm. "He doesn't change the situation, but he changes me. He gives me courage and strength. He gives me patient endurance. He gives me comfort and support. And when I need it most, he brings me peace. He does it without fail. And so I pray. And so he answers me." While I watched, Nicholas quietly nodded his assent.

I was lost in thought when Nicholas began to speak. "Christ told a story that emphasizes how God answers our prayers. And as I tell you the story, please remember that the Holy Spirit is the power of God that he gives us in answer to our prayers, just as Christopher said."

Nicholas paused and then continued. "Christ said to the people around him, 'If a child asks for bread, what father would give him a stone instead?' And then, in the same breath, Christ follows it with what he thinks is clearly the more important question: 'How much more will your Father in heaven give his Holy Spirit to those who ask him?'"

I considered this for a moment, and then Nicholas resumed. "When I think about God giving us his Holy Spirit, I wonder if there is a lesson to be learned from the story in the Bible in which Jesus quieted the wind and waves. The Bible tells us that the disciples were rowing across the Sea of Galilee, while Jesus was sleeping in the stern of the boat. The wind started to pick up, and pretty soon the disciples found themselves in the middle of a storm with the waves crashing against the boat."

I remembered the story well and listened on as Nicholas continued. "The disciples were desperate. I can imagine them huddled low in the boat, hanging on to the sides. Then they cried out to Jesus, 'Master, save us! We're going to perish!' This was, in fact, a prayer for help, perhaps the most desperate prayer of all. In response, Jesus stood up. Then he began talking to the wind and the waves."

I nodded, and Nicholas went on. "Remember, this was a rowboat. A large rowboat, but still a rowboat. If you have ever been in a rowboat in the middle of a storm, the last thing you do is stand up. The disciples must have been astounded. And then, as they saw Jesus standing in the boat as the storm raged around him, I can imagine the disciples taking heart, grabbing their oars, and rowing hard to bring their boat to the opposite shore,"

I smiled, and Nicholas continued. "Perhaps Jesus quieted the storm. He surely could do that. He could do any miracle that he wished. And the disciples were certain that he had indeed quieted the wind and the waves, and so it was recorded. But perhaps he did an even greater miracle and changed the disciples, changing their hearts and giving them courage and strength. As they looked at Jesus standing calmly in the boat, I can imagine them looking around and then looking at each other and saying, 'The waves don't seem so high anymore. The wind looks like it's dying down.' And so, pulling hard, they made their way to the safety of the shore."

As Nicholas paused, I took a moment to think. Then Nicholas went on. "If the wind lessened and the waves subsided, then Jesus gave the disciples safety for that night. Perhaps instead of changing the situation for a night, Jesus changed the disciples for a lifetime. They would face many perils. Perhaps each time, they would remember the storm. They would feel their courage rising, they would find their strength renewed, and they would make their way to safety."

I considered this carefully, then Nicholas continued. "Perhaps in every situation, the change God brings to our hearts is the greatest miracle of all. Here, let me give you an example. A mother is desperate, overcome by the death of her child. What would you want most for her? What would you pray for?"

I didn't answer. But Nicholas could see that he had my attention, so he went on. "What I would pray for, what I would want most for this mother, is that she can find peace, real peace. The child has died. I realize that I cannot change that. The grief will continue. Because her grief reflects the love the mother has for her child, I do not seek for that to go away. What I want most for that mother is that she finds peace, even while she carries her grief. If you think of that mother at peace, continuing to grieve, and yet at peace, you will sense what a rich blessing peace is and how worthwhile it is to pray for peace."

I looked at him and asked, "So how can you help her find peace?"

Nicholas nodded and then proceeded thoughtfully. "If that mother reaches out to God, he will help her find peace. Anytime we pray, God answers with the Holy Spirit, the power of God to change the heart." Nicholas could see me frown, so he gently touched my arm. Then he went on. "Follow this through, Hans. Please just listen a little more. The Holy Spirit brings the power of God to us, builds faith, and increases our faith. And as our faith grows, we find courage, determination, and, most importantly, peace. If we don't feel peace, keep praying. Relentlessly. And as we continue to pray, faith continues to grow, and eventually we will find peace. It is a prayer that God always answers. Always. Without fail."

I was deep in thought now as I turned and sat quietly in a nearby chair. I motioned to Nicholas to join me, hoping that he would stay longer. He sat, and together we watched my father holding Lenchen, gently talking to her. There was a sense of peace, just a hint perhaps, that seemed to hover over us.

The day passed slowly, as did the next day, the minutes ticking the hours away. One of us, and sometimes several of us, stayed close by Lenchen's side. My mother was often there. Her kindness and love were evident in the gentle hands that touched her child, her quiet voice soothing Lenchen. Aunt Lena came frequently as well. Despite her grief, she often wore a gentle smile, hoping to cheer Lenchen. And sometimes she was indeed rewarded with a smile, maybe just a hint, but a tiny smile nonetheless. More often, you could see the response in Lenchen's eyes…tired eyes that shifted slightly to focus on her mother or her aunt to show her love in turn. They even carried a faint sense of mischief when she looked at me. Or maybe I just imagined it. At thirteen, her sense of mischief was as much a part of her life as ever. It was embedded in her nature. Only her illness could limit its expression. At first it limited her plans and schemes, and now it limited the mischief in her eyes as well. Yet, I knew mischief was barely below the surface and would always be there, waiting for an ounce of strength to bring it to her eyes.

I talked with Lenchen often, telling her stories of my life at the university. Meaningless stories, really, but something to continue the bond that held us close, to keep a sense of communication between us. She found it hard to talk; it took so much effort just to breathe. But even an occasional word from her was a great reward.

My father frequently set aside his busy schedule to comfort her, to talk with her. He often left a peaceful child as he stepped away from her bedside. My father is a big man and carries a huge load, and yet the gentleness he brings to each visit touches all of us.

When others sit by her side, or when she sleeps, I often talk with Nicholas or Christopher, and many a time with both.

Tied to their studies, they still found time to sit with me as we watched Lenchen. Sometimes we saw her out of the corner of our eyes as she slept, and at times like these, I continued to talk to them about prayer. The conversation might be desultory, clouded by concern for Lenchen, yet gradually I came to understand more of what prayer can do.

"Nicholas, are you sure we shouldn't pray for things? Look, the Lord's Prayer says, 'Give us this day our daily bread.'"

Smiles were rare now, but still a gentle smile might come to the surface as it did now on Nicholas' face. "Surely you haven't forgotten what your father told us, Hans. God gives daily bread to the wicked as well as the good. When we pray this petition, it reminds us that the good in this world comes from God. And it reminds us to receive it with thanksgiving."

Without a pause, Nicholas went on. "We pray, 'Forgive us our sins, as we forgive those who sin against us.' We know that God has already forgiven our sins when Christ died on the cross. So when we pray this, we remind ourselves that forgiveness comes from God and how important it is that we forgive others."

I accepted this with the hint of a smile in turn. After a moment, Nicholas continued. "It's the same throughout the Lord's Prayer: 'Lead us not into temptation, but deliver us from evil.' As your father reminds us, God indeed tempts no one. But as we pray this, we are asking God to increase our resolve when we are faced with temptation. And each time we pray, we can feel our faith growing. We are stronger and more determined to do his will."

Often we sat quietly amid the grief. Then as we resumed

our quiet conversation, our voices were subdued, and Lenchen remained the focus. She was pale and weary, an even frailer figure on the bed. Worry for her, and our grief, turned the conversation often in her direction. Despair filled me as I looked at Nicholas, my voice barely audible as I choked on the words. "I can't bear to think of how sad it will be for Lenchen to leave us. I can try to deal with my own feelings, but I can't bear to think about her being sad."

Nicholas was thoughtful, his face grim, but his eyes remained steady. "Your father has worked a miracle. Or, rather, God has worked a miracle through your father. Remember how often he talked with her about peace? And explained how God has saved her and has her safely in his arms? Your father described for her how eternal life has already begun for each of us. Death for her will be like walking through a door. Her happiness will be greater than she can ever imagine. As he continues to come to her bedside, hold her, and talk with her, you can see that she is so openly at peace. The peace in his eyes, with her eyes fixed on him, clearly fills her soul as well. When you look at your father's face, you can see how terribly he feels the grief. And yet, his eyes are filled with peace, the peace of knowing that she will be happy. Happier than she can ever imagine."

Nicholas paused and then continued. "It is we who will be sad, Hans. Our sorrow in seeing her leave. But despite our sorrow, in our grief we can also find peace when we think of her happiness. And now, when we sit with her, she will sense our peace. And as she does, her sense of peace will increase as well. Peace now, and after she leaves, great happiness. That's the most we could ever wish for her."

I grew more thoughtful, less agitated. Then I turned abruptly to Nicholas. "How can she be happy while she's waiting to see us again? Won't she be lonely?"

Nicholas placed a gentle hand on my forearm. "Fortunately, Lenchen will not have to wait to see us. There is no waiting in heaven. Now, it's different for us. We will have to wait to see her again. For us, it will be hard. Because here on earth we live in time, the hours and days and years will have to pass for us before we get to see her again. But in heaven there is no time. Lenchen will not have to wait. We can't imagine eternity. But because our minds can only think in time, we can tell ourselves that in eternity a thousand years is like one second. In any case, for her, there is no waiting. We will wait, we will be sad, but we need never think that Lenchen will be sad or lonely."

As the days passed, I could feel the effect of my talks with Nicholas and Christopher. It started with a glimmer of peace, and as I prayed, it grew. When I found my turn to sit at Lenchen's bedside, I held her hand and talked quietly with her. My eyes held hers as well. Tears no longer filled my eyes as I increasingly found peace. My grief was intense, yet my face showed peace. And in her eyes, I could sense how my peace was met with peace in her as well. Deep peace and confidence showed in her face despite her struggle to breathe, to hang on to life.

I often sat beside her, holding her hand even while she dozed. And as I did, I considered again the conversations I had with Nicholas. I treasured my talks with Christopher as well, but it was Nicholas who came most often to mind. Peace was what I now wished most for Lenchen. I could not change the course of her illness. I couldn't bring color back to her cheeks, but I could help bring peace to her eyes.

I thought back to when I first heard my father bring peace as he talked with Lenchen. Now that I could feel peace, I hoped I could help my younger brothers and sister feel peace as well. As I talked to them at bedtime about Lenchen, I could sense an aura of peace surrounding us, or so it seemed to me. And as I searched their eyes and faces and listened to their conversation, I was certain that peace had clearly found its way into their lives.

One morning, as I thought about peace and how it is shared, I turned to Nicholas. I talked slowly as I felt my way, still thinking as the words came out. "I still have questions..."

Christopher walked in with my opening words, and with a gentle hand on my arm, he interrupted with a quiet smile. "We all do, Hans. I imagine even your father does."

I continued with a gentle smile in turn to welcome him. "Can you do more than pray for peace? For instance, if a mother has a sick child?"

Nicholas nodded. "It depends, Hans. If there is any chance that she can help her child who is ill or hungry or in any kind of danger, her first prayer must be something like this: 'Give me the courage, the determination, and the strength to never give up if there is something I can do to help my child...find food, to get care, anything.' But if, for instance, the child has an incurable illness and there is nothing she can do to affect the outcome, her prayer changes. 'Give me the courage and strength to bring comfort and peace to the one I love. Help him to know that he is not alone. That I am with him to hold him and comfort him. That God is with him and will walk with him hand in hand. That he will never be alone. And despite his pain now, there will be happiness. More happiness than he can ever imagine.'"

I nodded my head the slightest bit, enough to let him know that I was with him. Then slowly my mind moved on to another question. "If we're undecided about something, looking for answers, does God ever tell us what to do in response to our prayers?"

Nicholas was thoughtful, then responded. "This is the way I believe God helps me at a time like that. I pray God for courage, focus, and strength. Sometimes I pray for the determination to do what is right, even if it is not going to be easy. Sometimes I just ask that God will be with me as I find my way. Then, as I talk with God, I feel his presence. I feel my faith growing, and I feel God answering my prayer. I feel a strength within me that allows me to focus and dream and weigh. Yet, all the while, I know these are my decisions, the choices I make with my free will. And I know that I will need to live with the outcome of these decisions. That is the essence of free will…making choices."

I expect my face showed my concern. "But doesn't that make you uneasy, knowing it was your decision?"

Christopher was following the discussion and saw my concern. Now he broke in to re-emphasize what Nicholas had said. "Your faith will certainly help you in making a decision. Yet, you are the one who must make the choice. So this is what prayer will do, what faith will do. As you consider all the factors, God will help you to focus on what is important in your life. If you pray for God to help you, he will give you courage and strength. If you falter, faith gives you the determination to continue. Faith gives you strength to resist a temptation and courage to do what you know is right. And faith will help you to know that God will be with you whatever the outcome, and that makes all the difference. That is what allows me to move on with confidence."

I looked at one, then the other. "You certainly sound brave."

Nicholas shook his head, slightly but decisively. "Not at all. I pray so often the prayer of the man asking Jesus for help. When Jesus encouraged him to have faith, he replied, 'I believe, help thou my unbelief.' That's why I pray so often for faith."

After a pause, Nicholas continued. "And if it is a complicated situation and I am trying to find my way, I often remind myself of simple words of guidance in the Bible, and I apply them to myself. 'What does the Lord require of you, but to do justly, and to love mercy, and to walk humbly with your God.' Simple words, but they apply to so much of life."

Christopher added, "I may pray an even simpler prayer: 'Help me, Lord, to walk with you, every moment of every day, to walk with you.' Sometimes that's all it takes to help realign myself with what is important in life."

Another day passed, and as I entered the room, I realized that Lenchen was worse this morning. Her face was pale, her breathing ever more shallow now, as she lay quietly in her father's arms. I was wracked with grief, a term that barely begins to describe the terrible churning inside of me. My mother stood quietly beside Lenchen, her hands gently stroking her face, touching her hair, her hands never still. My mother's hands were soft, comforting, while her face was stricken, tears running down her cheeks. Aunt Lena stood nearby, her face contorted with grief. So often her contagious smile had brought cheer to those around her, but no more. Grief etched every corner of her face. Grief was on every face, reaching into every corner of the room. The only face that looked calm, peaceful, was Lenchen's.

I looked at her through tear-filled eyes. My gaze never left her face. Although I was heartbroken, my mind was registering every detail, recording every moment. Lenchen lay quiet, her breath increasingly shallow. Yet her eyes, though tired, still told of the confidence and peace she felt within. And as I watched her, I knew that everything Nicholas had said had come true.

I could not contain my grief, and neither could those around me. Yet the peace so evident in Lenchen's eyes revealed her confidence, her complete confidence, that she was passing through the door to eternal happiness. And that made all the difference. I knew that my grief would continue to be bitter, and I would have to deal with that. Yet, within me, in a tiny corner of my mind, was relief, almost a hint of joy, and a sense of victory that Lenchen need not share our grief. The peace my father first mentioned so many days ago had gradually become a deep sense of peace within Lenchen. Since I could not change the course of the illness, I knew that the peace that filled Lenchen was the greatest gift I could ever hope for. I understood now that it was peace that was the answer to my prayers. As I watched her lying in her father's arms, tired, yet so clearly at peace, Lenchen had achieved all I had prayed for.

Then, as I watched, the pattern of her breathing changed. Her breathing was more irregular now, becoming slightly erratic. And then a few halting breaths, a pause, one last breath, and all was still. Her face relaxed; she continued to be the picture of peace. She had passed through the door. She was incredibly happy.

I didn't think I would cry. I'm seventeen, after all. But to look at me is to see how red my eyes are now. I can hardly describe how I cried. Oh my, how I cried. Yet, when I had time to steady myself, I realized the sadness was for me, for us. For what we would be missing. As days passed, I also realized that I was not wishing for the grief to lessen. I didn't want to miss her less. I didn't want to have the terrible hole in my heart filled. I only hoped to manage my grief better.

Reminding myself that Lenchen was not grieving was a first big step. Reminding myself that Lenchen would not have to wait to see us again was just as important. Each of these brought the faintest sense of peace. I reminded myself that Lenchen was now happier than anything we can imagine. She was no longer struggling to catch her breath, no longer concerned about being ill. Days turned into weeks and months. A little more peace, very slowly, over time.

I sometimes wonder why Lenchen had such a powerful influence on me. Perhaps partly it was that at some level she sensed how serious her illness was. It did not dim her spirits. She was happy, mischievous, and active. But she carried a focus about life, about living fully, that was evident to those around her and that had a powerful effect on me. It was a sense of being true to herself, recognizing her frailties, accepting them but never letting them dominate her, and always searching for a way to find happiness. It was a trueness to herself that was probably most evident in her eyes.

Hopefully what I sensed in her will continue to be a spirit in me for the rest of my life. Then, if I also live true to myself, perhaps I will pass it on to those around me, those I love.

You ask me if the kitchen table is still the safest place on earth. Yes, it is. For in my memory, Lenchen still sits across the table from me, still gives me her mischievous grin. My father, still resolute, thoughtful, and confident, holds down the head of the table. My mother, comforting and supportive, sits close to me. Aunt Lena looks a little more worn, yet continues to bless us with her contagious smile. All the familiar faces are around the table. And in my memory, I continue to search out Nicholas as he sits across from me, but closer to my father.

Nicholas, my truest friend. My studies at the university keep my mind busy, occupied. Yet, in the quiet of the night, my mind reaches back to home, to family. My memories of Lenchen are bittersweet. There are moments of joy, and still the grief. I can feel, ever so slightly, an increase in the moments when I feel peace. It was you, Nicholas. You brought peace to my soul when I needed it most.

Now it's my turn to share. I need to find the words. My roommate is a restless soul. A true friend, thoughtful and kind, he carries a burden of his own. *Nicholas, he needs a friend like you.*

CHAPTER TEN

Hans Shares the Good News with Anthony

The university has now become my home. This little room may not look like much, but I'm eighteen and single and it fits me exactly. I spend much of my time studying. It's true. I'm comfortable among my books.

And yet, there's time, or at least I make time, to meet my friends wherever they gather, to talk, to laugh, and, more often than not, to get involved in vigorous debate. It doesn't take long before the air is thick with argument and counter-argument. Logic and reason prevail, and without these, an argument is readily dismissed. It's proof that is wanted if it can be obtained. We're scholars, after all, and nothing stands that is not supported by reason. The discussion is earnest and intense. But good will is a constant element and carries through the evening until we all depart as friends.

I arrived home late tonight, and the candle is burning low. My mind is gently summing up the day, ready to draw it to a close. I look forward to the comfortable bed that seems to be drawing me in. Then, a quick knock on the door, and in walks Anthony. I wasn't ready for such an abrupt change, but then nothing comes entirely as planned. Not in college, probably never in life.

It's time for bed. I have a lecture in the morning. But a friend is never turned away and is always welcome any time, even if the lack of sleep will cost me dearly in the morning… especially a friend who looks troubled, as Anthony does as he reveals what is most on his mind. His mother is old and seems to be failing fast. His father is worried and has reached out to him for support, something to help them find their way during this troubled time.

He ends his tale with this plea. "She's old, and I know there is nothing I can do to change the course of things. I wish I had faith, a way to comfort her. I wish I had your faith, Hans."

Faith, God, and eternity, these are topics that come to mind late at night. It may be that we carry these questions half-conscious in our souls and the deep hours of the night give us permission to talk of them to others. Questions of personal faith are not easy for me to discuss. I'm ready to give a gentle shrug and ease into a general discussion of parents and old age.

But Nicholas whispers to me quietly from one of our discussions years ago. "Here I am, Lord." Each word in this little phrase has a powerful message that speaks directly to me now. Here I am. Here, in this room, in the quiet of the night, with a friend who is searching for faith. Here I am. I am the one he came to, not another. Here I am. Present tense, now, at this moment.

Yet, I feel awkward, embarrassed even, to talk to another adult, a fellow student, about finding faith. For the only way to find faith is to approach the gospel with the open mind of a child. Anthony is immersed in the student's world of logic. He's thoughtful and well versed in philosophy. I find my mind searching for ways to avoid this discussion.

But Nicholas is persistent, and I cannot resist the voice echoing in my ear. "Here I am." I should not push it off into the future, perhaps to be forgotten. A friend has come to me asking for help. And Nicholas has helped me to understand that, "Here I am, Lord," is the only answer that my soul will permit.

So I begin slowly, feeling my way. "Well, you see, Anthony, it's rather a long story." I pause to see if he is ready or prefers to change the subject. He remains quiet, so I rise to find another candle, light it, and sit again, motioning Anthony to sit as well.

Then I begin again, cautiously, searching for words, a little pause between each phrase. "There's only one way to find faith. It's a clear path and easy to understand. But the difficulty is that it goes against every grain of our being."

Another pause, as I try to choose the right words. "You can't reason your way into finding faith. You can't study your way into it. The difficulty is you have to give yourself up, and just the sound of that turns so many away. We want to be in charge and do it ourselves. We want to do it the adult way, logically."

Anthony nods, waiting for me to continue, then urges me forward. "What should I do?" A brief pause, then, "What do you mean by giving myself up?"

Another pause as I struggle to find words that hopefully will not turn Anthony away. "You have to be willing to approach it with an open mind. Christ likens it to the open mind of a little child." Anthony doesn't move, looks thoughtful and relaxed.

I find the words coming easier now. "Look, Anthony, your mind will resist. It will insist on addressing it as a matter of logic, looking for proof. Your soul, your being, will resist. It will do everything it can to avoid being seen as a child. It embarrasses us terribly if we think of doing something that makes us look so naïve, so childish."

I pause again to let Anthony move off the subject, but Anthony looks intent on hearing me out, so I continue. "Christ was very specific when he talked with his disciples. You must become like a child. If you approach the gospel with the open mind of a child, a mind that is ready to accept, then God will instill faith. And as you continue to read or listen, you will feel your faith growing. It will take time. You must be persistent. But as long as you keep an open mind and continue to approach the gospel, faith will come. At first there will be doubts, but then faith grows. And eventually, by faith, we listen to the good news and know it to be true."

Anthony looks thoughtful and I am grateful that he did not shrug me off at the mention of a child. Instead, Anthony surprises me by pushing me onward. "What do you mean by 'approaching the gospel'?"

The words come easier, and I explain that the gospel is the good news" of our salvation. Then I point out that before you can know that you've been saved, it's important to know that you were lost. I talk to him about man's ability to choose between good and evil and how he yielded to temptation and chose evil, as we so often do ourselves. I discuss some of the results of evil that surrounds us, disease, war, famine, starvation. And finally, I point out that without Christ we each of us have lost eternal life. I talk about eternal death and what it means. My voice is kind, yet I do not skirt the issue. I emphasize the fact that we were doomed, that we walked in darkness and in the shadow of death.

I wait to see how he responds, but Anthony makes no reply and instead looks patiently at me, willing for me to continue. And so I talk of the 'good news' that comes to us in the gospel. How God saved us by sending his Son and how Christ saved us by taking on himself the punishment for our sins. I emphasize that saved from our sins, we have eternal life. We no longer walk in the shadow of death. Christ has brought us out of the darkness and into the light. We know that in the end there will be happiness, more happiness than we can ever imagine. And in that knowledge, we are at peace with God and with ourselves.

Anthony is impressed, but I can sense a lingering doubt. He wants to know his part, what he can do. I smile, just a gentle smile, understanding his struggle, like the struggle of all of us who want so much to take things into our own hands and exercise some control. Then I point out that salvation is God's free gift to man. Man doesn't contribute in any way. All we can do is to thank him.

As we talk on through the night, Anthony presses me for guidance—for specifics. We talk of reading the gospels. The central message in each gospel is the same—each one telling the story of our salvation. Yet each one helps us to appreciate what the good news means by telling the same story from a different viewpoint. The book of Acts tells us how the disciples responded to the good news and spread the word, the story of the early church. The epistles are letters encouraging the early believers, discussing how this good news fits into their lives and into our lives as well.

As the minutes and then the hours passed, we came again to his concern for his mother.

"But what does this mean to her? How will it help her?"

I find myself reaching deep inside to memories that are cherished, yet carefully guarded. We talk of peace as we face death. "When you can sense that she's at peace, you'll realize what a great gift that is for her."

Anthony is thoughtful, and I sense he may be agreeing. I hope he is. It's hard to tell, as he asks what he can do to help her feel at peace. I reach out to touch his forearm as I reply. "Tell her how much God cares for her. Tell her that he's by her side. That he will hold her hand. Tell her the story of salvation. Tell her that he has already saved her, has freed her from any worry about death. Tell her that death is a doorway to great happiness."

I pause for a moment, then add, "You'll probably feel uneasy talking about God. But if you have the courage and approach it gently, you may be rewarded with a response. You may see her becoming more peaceful, especially if she sees in your eyes how much you care and sees in your face the confidence you have in what you are saying to her. Hopefully, she will see that you also feel at peace. If she wants to know more, she will ask."

Another pause follows, and then I continue. "Don't worry. At that point, you will find the answers. Keep reminding her how much God loves her and how he has her in his care. You will be able to sense from her attitude how best to express yourself. But don't lose the courage to reach out. You may be so surprised to see how much this means to her. And you may find yourself so grateful that you did. Remember, this will be your chance. Later, if you wish you had, you will think of it with regret."

Anthony remains quiet, so in a moment, I continue. "And if you see your mother is at peace, you will realize that this is, indeed, the answer to your prayers."

By now, it's close to dawn. Soon the sun will bring its light to dispel the darkness. Anthony tells me of his plans to travel to his mother's home later that day. In a moment of quiet between us, I notice his face shows how tired he is. A look at his eyes, and I can sense how his eyes demand sleep. And still his friendship, his gratitude, are evident as he turns to me for a moment before leaving. He looks at me and then gives a nod, his eyes friendly.

I nod as well, our way of acknowledging the bond between us. As I walk with him to the door I add, "I'll go with you to the coach stop later this morning. I'll see you off." His face relaxes and he almost smiles as he turns to go.

As the door closes, I say, "Thank you, Nicholas. I owe this to you. A little more light in the darkness."

Hopefully for Anthony, it is a step that will bring him

courage, strength, and, most of all, peace. Just one person, just a start. But I hope it means as much to Anthony as it means to me. I hope he continues onward. In the faint light of dawn, I can sense Nicholas glancing back at me with a smile that reflects our friendship and his own pride for having prepared me for this moment.

A few hours later I'm in class. My red eyes will suggest to my professor that I have had a night of drinking. Actually, it's been much better. I'm not sure what Anthony's plans are to help his mother in her final days. Yet, I'm certain we are better friends for the night we spent talking. And I'm grateful for that.

When class is over, I'm off to see Anthony and walk him to the carriage. I'll start him on the journey that will take him home to see his mother. When I get to his apartment, I find that he has already gone. I'm sure I can catch up with him since he has a piece of luggage to contend with. Sure enough, I see him up ahead, and in a few minutes, I fall in step with him.

It's difficult for me to sense his mood. He's certainly thoughtful, knowing what lies ahead. But he looks a little more confident than he did last night, or so I imagine. We talk quietly about his mother's illness, the despair so evident in his father's letters, and the many difficulties of caring for parents at this time in their lives.

As we approach the place where Anthony will catch the carriage, we see that it is already in place. It will take a few minutes to bring up a fresh team of horses, so we sit side by side on a fence rail. We don't talk much at this point, but I take a couple moments to glance at him as he stares thoughtfully at the coach. As I consider what lies ahead, I wish with all my heart that his journey will go well.

I throw an arm lightly over his shoulder. He responds with a rueful smile that expresses the sorrow and worry that he carries with him. Then, side by side, we walk slowly to the coach. As we get to the step, I can see he is searching for words. We pause for a moment, but words won't come. Silently, he puts his foot on the carriage step. Then, as he turns to enter, I hear the simple word "thanks" escape from his lips. If his thanks is for the small amount of peace that I have shared, he is indeed very welcome. Perhaps it is for the peace he feels and the peace he wishes to share. If that's his hope, it is my fervent prayer.

Back in my room, I look around, remembering our long discussion of the night before. Another prayer forms in my mind. "Thank you, God, for giving me the courage and strength to talk with Anthony. Where it will lead only you know. But maybe Anthony will bring a little light into a darkened household." Then, with a hint of a smile, I add, "And thank you, Nicholas. You so often spoke of spreading the good news to the ends of the earth. Well, this is a start. This is where I am."

As I think of Nicholas, my heart grows lighter. *You were so often by my side when most I needed you. I owe so much to you, my friend and mentor. And now I only wait to hear the outcome. My hope is that the peace that you brought me brings peace as well to Anthony. And perhaps beyond.*

CHAPTER ELEVEN

Anthony Shares It Further

Weeks have passed, and once again, I heard a welcome knock at my door. It was a long-awaited knock, for Anthony has been often on my mind. As he came through the door, I noticed how tired and how worn he looked. And yet, he had an unmistakable air of quiet confidence about him. I even sensed that he was more at peace, at least I hoped so. I'd have to see.

He clearly wants to tell me how it went, and so we settle into chairs and he begins to talk. I'll just give you the highlights. This is what he told me. His story, and in his words:

> You can't believe how deeply my father was distressed, my mother troubled, restless. It seemed to me there was a heavy layer of weariness that covered them and added to their burden. It was evident in their words, their

attitude, the way my father walked, and the way my mother's hands moved noiselessly among the covers of her bed, refusing to be still. She was attempting to hold on to life, but her grasp was weak and tenuous.

"It wasn't supposed to end like this," my father said.

I certainly agreed, and somehow the knowledge of this gave me the courage to begin. "It doesn't have to," I assured them. "God is with us, in this room. He brings peace, the comfort of knowing we are not alone, the sure knowledge that we have each been saved."

"Saved from what?" my father asked, the question short and dismissive.

So I started at the beginning, and this is what I said. "God gave man the ability to choose between good and evil. When man chose evil, a whole host of evils came into the world. Even worse, man could no longer look forward to eternal life. Man lived in the shadow of death."

"Stop," my father said. "Please stop. You can see you're frightening your mother."

And, indeed, the anxiety so evident on her face had increased. Her eyes were dull and distant. She needed to hear the good news.

So I told them how God took everything into his own hands. He sent his Son to die for us, to pay the penalty for our sins. He died for each of us, for all of us. He died for the sins of the whole world, and he brought eternal life for everyone. Now death is but a doorway. We have eternal life; we face eternal happiness. All this a free gift from God. We did nothing to deserve it, and we can do nothing to earn it. There is nothing we can do to pay God back for what he has done. All we can do is say thank you.

Each day I repeated the good news, telling it in simple terms, assuring my mother that she was safe and, that she would be happier than she could ever imagine. And gradually, day by day, she watched me with more interest. Her face showed less anxiety and began to show signs of peace, or so it seemed to me.

Meanwhile, my father was reluctant. "Are you trying to make believers out of us? Is this your way of saving us?"

I assured my father that, in fact, I was not trying to save them. God had already done that. Being saved is not up to us; it's up to God.

"But tell me, Anthony, what happens if I don't believe?" my father asked.

"God has saved all of us, each of us," I replied. Then I assured him, "Even if you don't believe, you can't undo what God has done for you."

There was a pause, yet I could sense that they were listening. So I continued. "But this is what believing does," I told them. "Believing brings us now the sure knowledge that we have been saved. Believing means we no longer live in the shadow of death. Believing means we know we have eternal life. Believing means our death is but a doorway leading to eternal happiness. Believing allows us to live in peace with God and with ourselves."

The days went by, and I saw a little more peace on my mother's face and a little less challenge on my father's part. The questions now reflected his need for answers. Answers to my mother's illness and answers to their future.

"Are you asking us to look to God for help?" he asked. "What has he done for us?"

"We should always look to God for help," this I assured him. "The diseases of old age are not likely to go away," I gently told him. "And my mother is not likely to get well," I advised him in an even gentler voice. "But God is surely bringing peace to her. And every time we look to God and ask God for help, his answer to our prayer is to assure us that we are not alone. He is with us and has us by the hand. We look to God in any way we can, through prayer, by reading what he has done, and by listening. Each time there is an answer, an increase in our faith."

"Sometimes I get overwhelmed by all that I was taught," my father said. "I have put nearly all of that behind me."

"If you look back at what you have been taught and if you find it strengthens your faith, then it is serving you well," this I assured them both. "If not, do not let it distract you from the central message, a message so clear. Christ has saved you from your sins, saved all of us. He has given us eternal life. And when we die, eternal happiness. Never lose sight of this. If the rest helps you, all the better. But never let it cloud the message of our salvation. If you find this difficult, if you are struggling to choose Christ, remember that he has already chosen you."

A few more days, time to sit for hours at my mother's side. At times to talk with her, at times to sit quietly, and at times to hold her hand. And always to see signs of peace on her face, in her attitude. And early signs of peace in my father's face, as well.

"I can't believe it's supposed to end like this," he said once more.

"It isn't, really," I replied, taking the opportunity to talk again of eternal life, eternal happiness, adding to our previous discussions, slowly building toward the time when faith becomes sure knowledge.

I was feeling more relaxed and more at peace now. Perhaps my face showed it, because there was peace reflected in their faces as well. Just a little, but peace nonetheless. And it seemed that it was growing day by day. At least I hoped so. That was my prayer.

"Is there nothing I must do?" my father asked. I pointed out that God had done it all. All we can do is say thank you. The love we feel is best expressed in what we do for those we love, for others close at hand and strangers anywhere in need.

Eventually, I left my parents' side to return to the university and to make up for all that I had missed. But I'll go back again. I made a start; I'm sure of that. My parents are different now than when I first arrived. When peace finds its way into our souls, it reaches everywhere and changes the atmosphere. It affects everything we do in life, how we feel about ourselves, how we relate to others. And most of all, it brings the confidence with which we face the future. I sense I have made a beginning. And I will build on that.

Anthony was relaxed now, reflecting on his visit for a moment. Then he continued in a voice of quiet confidence. "Looking back, I must admit I was afraid," he acknowledged, glancing sideways at me. "I was unsure of what to say, embarrassed in a way. And now my prayer is only that I find the courage to continue." He paused for a moment. "My parents need my help." Then turning to look fully at my face, he continued. "And I need yours."

I smiled and nodded, indicating I would gladly help him. Then I added, "You already know the way." I paused for a moment and then continued. "And I will help you in any way

I can." It was a promise I could keep. In the very least, with encouragement and support.

Later, sitting quietly in the silence of my room, I thought of Nicholas. *I never knew, Nicholas, that what you told me in answer to my questions was not just mine to keep, but rather mine to share. I passed it on to Anthony, he to his parents. No way to know where it will end, if it will end at all.*

In fact, Nicholas, as I look far and wide, I'm sure that it will never end. The words you shared with me, the good news that you spoke of, continues to be spread by many, continues to reach outward to the ends of the earth. Each of us is just one voice joining in the chorus.

CHAPTER TWELVE

Now It's Our Turn

The longer I'm away from home, the more I relish the times when my mind drifts home to memories of family. Inevitably, they are seated at the kitchen table, still the safest place on earth. There is the comfortable intensity of eager conversation. The air that surrounds my family is charged with enthusiasm, contentment, and, best of all, with total acceptance. This air, this atmosphere, assures me of my place within the family. It makes me feel incredibly safe.

My mind drifts round the table. My father is expressing his position on faith with insight and clarity. When discussion becomes heated, it still projects a sense of mutual respect and is often interspersed with humor. My father is in charge and never lets a hint of anger enter the debate. I love my father dearly and respect him even more. He has a natural air of authority and confidence that add greatly to my sense of safety while seated at the table.

At my end of the table, my mother brings a warm, enduring love that envelops me securely. At times consoling, when I was younger and things had gone wrong. At times pushing me gently forward, when I was hesitant to take a path that would be difficult, yet one I knew was right for me. She is often busy, her labors focused on providing for the needs of the family, for each of us. From every angle, she brings a sense of comfort and safety to the table.

Glancing up I get a smile from Aunt Lena, a smile reserved for children she has known from little on. *You have nurtured me, Aunt Lena. When I was a child, your lap provided a secure and comfortable home. Each of my faults is clearly known to you, as you have watched me grow to young adult. Faults I have resolved and those that linger still, you know each one. Yet your smile says, "I accept you, totally, completely, with all my heart." The smile confirms our relationship. You share it with others, yet when your smile draws me in, I feel it is a smile reserved for me.*

I wait to catch Nicholas's attention, and when I do, I smile and nod my head to invite him to help me understand the issues in the conversation that swirls around me. Sometimes I can sense the value of the point at hand and sometimes not. In any case, Nicholas can always clarify and simplify the discussion in a way that allows me to weigh the issues and consider where they take me. *Nicholas, you have helped me to make sense of the world around me and within me. You, too, have added to the safety of the kitchen table.*

My mind at ease drifts comfortably and then changes course abruptly. How can I feel happiness when Lenchen is no longer here among us? I look across the table and there, to my surprise, I see Lenchen with a smile that reaches out to capture every corner of her face. Then she breaks into a laugh. My heart is filled to overflowing as I take her laughter in. She laughs so hard that I see tears of joy that glisten in her eyes. She looks directly at me as her laughter confirms that she knows happiness greater than she had ever imagined. *Lenchen, you have always been my lodestone and now my picture of eternal happiness.* Probably many have a different picture of heaven, but Lenchen is a child. Her happiness is evident in her laugh and in her eyes.

Once again, with laughter shared, I glance around the kitchen table, treasuring the atmosphere of mutual acceptance. From the safety of our kitchen table, I learned so much about life, so much about God. My heart is full, and I am at peace.

Then from the corner of my eyes, I see Nicholas looking quietly, intently in my direction. His manner suggests that he is searching for something more, waiting for me to take another step. I sift through all the memories that the kitchen table and my family bring to mind. I look for clues, think carefully about where those thoughts may lead, trying to sense where Nicholas is guiding me. Carefully, I think again about the safety that I cherish so.

Suddenly, it comes to me. I realize that I am always young in my memories of the kitchen table. And now, having gathered so much from the safety of that table, there is much I need to do. All I have learned is now mine to apply. The safety of the kitchen table gives me courage. The good news of our salvation gives me purpose.

Christ died to save me from my sins and to earn for me eternal life, eternal happiness. And now I am at loss. It was a free gift from God. Totally free. We didn't earn it, we don't deserve it, and we cannot pay him back. So there we are, with nothing in our hands. And yet, there is much that we can do.

For now it's our turn, the turn that comes to each of us. We can say thank you. We can say it in our words, and we can say it in our lives. The love we feel for all that has been done for us is best expressed in reaching out to others. We reach out with words of love and friendship. We reach out by sharing what we have. And most of all, we reach out by spreading the good news, the news of our salvation, the news of eternal life and happiness.

I dream of doing something big, something special. Yet, I am reminded that this is where I am. Make every effort, I remind myself, to do what best I can and to look for ways to show my love for others. For there is much that can be done. Perhaps it is a smile to relieve another's loneliness. Perhaps it will be more. We each will find within ourselves how best we show that love. The importance is in reaching out. Eternal life, eternal happiness, and peace are ours…ours to have and ours to share.

We each can say there's someone else I can tell. This is where I am. This is what I can do. It's not the end. Not yet.

EPILOGUE

God has us by the hand.
Faith helps us to know that.

Discussion Questions for Readers

Chapter One: So This Is Faith

1. Does the kitchen table in this home seem like a safe place to you?
2. Would you like to grow up in the household that Hans has? Do you think that would be a good preparation for life?
3. If you encountered an angel, would you react like Zechariah or like Mary? Which would you prefer?
4. Do you admire Mary's faith?
5. Do you wish you had a stronger faith?

Chapter Two: We Were Accountable

1. If you laugh with others, does that make you feel a bond? How important is it to have laughter in a household?
2. Do you wonder where evil comes from? Do you agree with Nicholas that no one wants to talk about it?

3. Do you believe that man's choice of evil is the cause of all the evils in this world? If so, do you think this is fair?
4. Does it make you angry with God when you think of all the evils in this world? Do you think it is fair to be angry?
5. Do you feel God is on our side as we deal with the evils in this world? If so, can you give an example from your life?

Chapter Three: We Are Forgiven

1. Do you think the preaching and miracles Jesus did would convince you that he was the Son of God if you lived in those days?
2. Does it seem reasonable to you that God would forgive the sins of everyone when his Son died on the cross?
3. Do you agree with Nicholas that in all of history, Christ's death on the cross on that dark afternoon was the most important moment for each of us?
4. Was it the most important moment for you?
5. Do you find that being assured of eternal life and happiness allows you to live in peace? Does it allow you to feel comfortable about facing death?

Chapter Four: Grace, A Gift from God

1. Do you agree with Nicholas that faith comes to us if we approach the gospel with an open mind? Do you agree with him that this is the only way we find faith?

2. Do you agree with Christopher that being open-minded may sound easy, but coming with an open mind is really the difficult part? Do you agree that we pride ourselves with being open-minded, but at the same time, we want anything of importance to be supported by reason?
3. Do you agree that worries and cares head the list of things that distract people from their faith? Do worries and cares head the list for you?
4. Do you agree that forgiveness, salvation, eternal life, and even faith are all gifts from God? And that he gives these freely to us, with no strings attached?

Chapter Five: We Say Thank You

1. Do you agree with Nicholas that we thank God by showing that we love him? And that the best way to show our love for God is to love our neighbor?
2. Do you agree that love is an action word, more than a warm feeling? And that we show our love by what we do more than by saying how we feel?
3. Do you agree with Christopher that one way of helping our neighbor is not judging him? Do you feel we can show our love by condemning the sin while being kind to the sinner?
4. Do you find that sometimes you make demands on yourself that you would never ask of someone else? Do you believe it is important that you love yourself as you do your neighbor?
5. Do you find that the opportunity to love someone is the greatest gift they can give you?

Chapter Six: We Are Inspired

1. Do you agree with Nicholas that it is clear that the Bible is inspired because it is so clear that the Bible inspires us? If so, do any of you wish to mention your own experience?
2. Do you agree with Nicholas that hearing four people tell the story of salvation, each from his own viewpoint, adds strength to the message, rather than having just one account? Do you agree that variation in detail from witnesses is what you would expect and makes the basic story more believable? If so, do any of you have similar experiences?

Chapter Seven: Interactions with God

1. Do you agree with Nicholas that baptism is a personal interaction with God in which the words assure me that my sins are washed away, emphasized, and made personal by the water which washes me?
2. If you recall your baptism, do you feel this personal interaction with God and assurance of forgiveness? If you were to be baptized, do you think baptism would have this effect on you?
3. Do you agree with Nicholas that the Lord's Supper is a personal interaction with God in which the words assure me that my sins are forgiven, while the bread and wine make this personal and give me a powerful reminder of how Christ sacrificed himself to earn my salvation?

4. Do you feel that Lenchen's questions about the sun are what you might expect from a nine-year-old child who is frequently ill and who may feel some question about her future? If so, do you feel Lenchen is brave in the way she faces this question about her future?
5. Do you feel the close bond between Hans and Lenchen and enjoy the gentle attempts of each to exert authority over the other? Do you have such a relationship in your life?

Chapter Eight: The Church Spreads the Good News

1. Do you agree with Nicholas that the role of the church is to strengthen the faith of believers and spread the good news to the ends of the earth?
2. Do you agree with Christopher that the role of missionaries is to bring light to people in darkness, not to save them from hell?
3. Do you think it is worth sending missionaries to the ends of the earth to bring people out of darkness and out of the shadow of death?
4. Do you agree that the best description of heaven is being happier than anything you can imagine?

Chapter Nine: God Answers Prayer

1. Do you pray that God will help you make a decision? If so, perhaps you might pray for God to give you a sign. Or perhaps you might pray for God to give you focus, courage, and strength that will help you make a

decision that is totally yours. If you do, what influences your preference?

2. Nicholas told Hans that when a loved one dies, while we will be sad, the loved one will be happier than we can imagine. Do you agree with Nicholas? If so, does this help you in dealing with the loss of a loved one?

3. Nicholas told Hans that while we will have to wait to see our loved one again, our loved will not have to wait to see us because there is no time in eternity. Do you agree with Nicholas? If so, does this help you in dealing with the loss of a loved one?

4. Do you know someone like Lenchen who has a serious illness and yet rises above it to focus on the happiness to be found in life? If so, does that help you to deal with life?

Chapter Ten: Hans Shares the Good News with Anthony

1. Do you find, as Hans did, that it is easier to talk with friends about faith, God, and eternity in the late hours of the night? If so, what do you think there is about the late hours of the night that makes this so?

2. Hans heard Nicholas encouraging him to help Anthony. Have you ever had the sense that someone was encouraging you to do the right thing when you were reluctant? If so, can you share that?

3. Hans felt awkward, embarrassed even, to talk to another adult about finding faith. If you share those feelings, why do you think that is so?

Chapter Eleven: Anthony Shares It Further

1. Anthony says he felt unsure, embarrassed in a way, as he began to talk with his parents. Do you think you would have felt the same way? If so, how would you have gathered the courage to continue?
2. Hans thought back to the many questions he had for Nicholas and how he now realized the answers were not just his to keep but his to share. Do you agree with Hans that we have an obligation to share with others if someone has shared something helpful with us?

Chapter Twelve: Now It's Our Turn

1. Hans has learned so much from Nicholas, and now he feels the need to pass on what he has learned. Have you ever had a similar experience?
2. Do you agree with Hans that each of us knows best how we can show God's love?